# Two Moons

### Stories

# Two Moons: Stories

Krystal A. Smith

PRESS

Clayton, NC

Printed in the United States of America

First Printing, 2018

Cover Art: Mirlande Jean-Gilles
Cover Design: Lauren Curry

ISBN Print: 978-0-9972439-0-1
ISBN Ebook: 978-0-9972439-1-8
Library of Congress Control Number: 2017954672

BLF Press
PO Box 833
Clayton, NC 27520

www.blfpress.com

# Contents

# Search

Travel to the desert town of Orko. Go seven miles past Gladys'
roadside ice cream stand. Find the blooming willow acacia tree
in the empty field where long wild grasses grow. You'll know it
by the silvery blue leaves tipped up toward the sky drinking in
the plum moon. One of its wispy branches points out into the
darkness, a gnarly finger your guide.

Walk in the direction it leads. But do not be fooled.
Darkness is everywhere. Tonight you head north toward
Truth. Don't let the night birds distract you with their songs.
"Shoop, shoop, shoop. Hey, hey, hey! Where you going?
Gimme yo' number. Shoop, shoop, shoop." Even if they say
something about yo' mama, keep walking. St. LaDonta knows
why you have come, even if you don't, and she's waiting
for you.

Take careful steps, make your body in each one, leave
nothing behind in five hundred moves.

A quarter of a mile and you have arrived. Read the
ground. Trust that you know how. See its breath? Yes, you
do. Pieces of rust colored glass blend into the earth at your

feet. Empty your pockets. Drop everything to the desert floor. Everything. Your lip balm, the loose change of quarters, one dime, and three pennies you've been carrying just in case, your Grapevine video rental card. Give it all as an offering. Drag your right foot across the dirt in front of your left to mark time. Tick, tick, tick, tick, tick. Now pick up a single piece of glass and carve your names backwards in the ground. SUNEV. KCALB. NAMOW. REGNARTS. REVOL. Spit an exclamation mark into your left hand then touch the edge of glass with dirt on it to your palm.

Say nothing. Wait.

St. LaDonta prepares for you. She's heard you whispering to yourself for a long time. *Are you enough, are you, are you, are you? Why are you this way, why, why, why?* You should know by now why you've come all this way. Think. Why have you come? She will ask you and you must tell her.

Orange dust starts to rise. It brushes up against your sneakers and jeans. It settles in your hair, painting a halo on your Afro. The ground trembles then rolls in big looping waves like the colorful parachute you played under in school. Remember? "Run under, children. Look underneath." Mrs. Jones grabbed your end and let you run inside the giant chute. You found big air. You couldn't stop your eyes from growing wide or your breath from clogging up your throat and for the first time you believed in space to breathe, in a place you could belong, in magic.

You've closed your eyes to remember Mrs. Jones and the chute and how time can be still. But don't take too much longer on your memory.

Open your eyes!

St. LaDonta!

Deepest black. Cool black. Shadow black. Changeling black. Femme feminine black. Soft black. Hungry black. Black black St. LaDonta.

See how she stands in front of you with her mouth open and ready, her head tilted all the way to the side. See her look you over with wide eyes made of black pearly buttons that nearly touch into one. Look back at her. Stare. Take her in. It's all right. What do you see? Hair made of long, glossy, black spider webs collecting knowledge, secrets. Black conch shell lips warning, informing, feeding you. An oil filled belly sets the temperature for your womb. Fiyah. Fiyah. Fiyah. What do you sense? Why have you come?

Look at her. Look closer. See her.

Raise your right hand to the sky. Watch her hand shoot up into the atmosphere and ring the moon. Tap your left foot to the ground. Feel the cool waters below, stirred by her flat foot. Do you understand now? Do you know who you are?

Hear her voice rush out like wind, notice her golden tongue punctuate and taste the air.

Speak to her your reasons, your wants, your needs. Why have you come? Do you know?

Tell her.

Tell her now.

Hesitation does not serve you. It will never serve you.

Speak!

You are here. You made this journey. You are worthy. You will be replenished. Place your hand between her wild claws.

Feel the heat, the energy she pumps and flows into you. She fills you with Fiyah!

She strips you down, frees you, shows you yourself, your splendor. She presses your skin into thin black sheets, whips damp stardust and dried clay and flowers and healing water into your cracks and crevices.

She swallows you whole then bleeds you out.

Cry! Cry! Smack your lips, gnash your teeth, tear out your hair until all that's left is ground moss and velvet birds' feathers.

Ask for forgiveness.

Ask for love, for knowledge, for safety, for sturdier bones, for more flesh. Whatever it is, grant yourself the ask. Fall to your knees and thank her, thank her a thousand times until your tongue dries out and hardens into bone, until it turns gold and black with bruises and understanding.

Let the ground soak a circle of jeweled tar around your body. Lie in it, roll in it. You have been searching for a way, a way, a way to become your own. To become deepest black, warmest black, sun-lit black, mascu-femmie black, hardest and softest black, open black, your black, your blackest black.

Unfold yourself back together; don your clothes piece-by-piece, smooth out the wrinkles in your heart and mind. Snatch at the wind with your giant gaping mouth. Feed until you are fat and luscious with earthly ingredients. Fill yourself with bulbous cloud membranes, then blow across the desert spreading your seed, your new light.

You can fly now. Fly.

# Anyone Out There

**Started in 2025, the Any Love Project was a video matchmaking platform for single people seeking a real connection. The videos were shot into space to save cloud storage at the expansion and purchased by the Solar Mining Group for the cadets surveying the outer limits.**

Josie floated the one-person pod capsule into Nebula Twelve docking station for rations. She had a video playing on the center module screen between a map of Ultimate Nine space cloud and a picture of the original navigation crew. Josie missed her home planet and sunshine and shea butter deep conditioning lotion. The only extravagance that didn't take up space in the pod was Cora's video playing on loop in the solar deck.

The face on screen looked at Josie straight on. Mercury gray eyes, a wide nose with a mole nestled in the corner, and honey brown lips filled the screen. Josie often held the video at the 00:01:15 mark just to stare back at the smiling face. It was the most intimate moment in space.

The beginning was Josie's favorite. The way Cora's voice started off so confident made Josie forget she was floating in a body capsule with only the necessary room to move. Cora's voice filled the cabin and made it home.

*Here goes. Hi. I'm Cora Rayne. Spelled R-A-Y-N-E though I'm quite fond of precipitation. I sleep really great when it rains. I wake up so refreshed, you know, like my body synced up with nature. You don't have to be a deep sleeper or a light sleeper... Just however you sleep is fine. Well, you can see already that I tend to ramble. So, you should be able to keep me on track or not mind if I ramble. Either or both would probably be good.*

*I'm looking for someone who is kind. I know people say that all the time, but really, what do we have if we don't have kindness? I think the best way to be kind is to show consideration. We are so busy with inane things we hardly stop to consider how we affect the people around us. Animals too. I think we should have kindness for animals, all creatures. There's a metal railing outside my apartment building where lots of little birds like to perch and sing. They bring in the morning that way. The sound is beautiful. I love to listen to them. But when it gets cold the metal railing freezes and if the birds stop for a quick song and sit too long their little feet stick to it. My neighbors walk by and I wonder how they can just walk by. These birds sing and we get to delight in that song. I saw a bird frozen to that railing just the other day and I couldn't walk by. I would want someone to stop for me. I didn't have anything in my hands to help the little bird. But then I realized I had my hands and my breath. So, I cupped my hands around the bird. A little gray thing, I don't know what kind, and I blew my warm breath on its feet. I know I looked a fool to my neighbors, but in that there was kindness. The bird flew away with both its feet though. So to me that was success in kindness… I'm rambling again.*

Josie didn't mind the rambling. It helped her bide time while surveying. Space mining was a thoughtless job. She missed birds. She'd always been afraid of them on land. Their eyes were so focused. Like they were reading data from people's minds. But now she made herself think of them. When she got back, she'd volunteer at a sanctuary. If sanctuaries were still around when she returned. Four years left on her mining contract meant a lot would be different on the ground in 2043.

*You could like music. All kinds. Music tells a story. I like to think stories heal. And music can best describe how we feel at a given time, often much better than words. Music is mathematical which means music is also logical. So music is good.*

Josie picked up her drill scope like a microphone. "On our first date we could listen to something sweet and romantic, something that warranted holding each other close, cheek to cheek, torso to torso. We could talk with our measured breath. Luther Vandross. "Any Love" that would heal us both. She hummed into the head of the scope.

*I'm a crier. I've finally gotten comfortable with that. I'm a real person with real emotions. I'm sensitive. If I can't cry in front of you, it'll never work. I was with someone for a while who, whenever I got emotional or cried would say to me, 'What are you crying about now?' And the way she said it made me feel as if something was wrong with me. That hurt me. Deeply. I know I don't want that again. I don't always know what to say* when other people are crying, but I won't leave the room. I won't leave you alone, unless that's what you need. I can sit quietly with you until you're ready to speak.

Quiet time is important. We can be quiet separately or together. I think that would be neat. Just sitting together, enjoying each other's silence. You can learn a lot about someone that way.

Josie always laughed at this part, 00:04:05. Quiet time. All Josie had was quiet time. All day, every day. Sometimes the sound of her own voice was too quiet, blending into the nothingness all around. "If quiet time was a game, I'd freakin' win so hard. I can give you quiet time. Whenever, wherever. Maybe we could make a trade off. You can have quiet Tuesday/Thursday and I can have raucous noise, music, drums, air breaks, and dogs barking Monday/Wednesday. Would that work?"

Hmm, what else? Oh, sex. I don't possess an uncontrollable drive, but I'd say my appetite is healthy. I've had four, no, um, five intimate partners. I'm no stranger to experimenting. I figure as long as everyone is consenting, upfront, and honest, sex can be a powerful tool for bringing people together. And it's fun, it feels good.

"My appetite is healthy," Josie repeated, trying to digest just what that meant. The first time she watched the video Josie fixated on four words, *experimenting, fun, feels good.*

Emotional and physical intimacy is important to me. Hold my hand, tell me what scares you, make me laugh until my voice goes up into the high-pitched wheezing laugh. Let's create our own language. Teach me how to do something you do well. Let *me read to you before we fall asleep. I feel like I'm leaving out so much, but I guess the recording can only be so long.*

*Don't touch my feet. Not even in a playful way. I really dislike my feet being touched. You don't have to challenge me and see if I really don't like it or if I'm angling for a foot massage. Really. Don't touch 'em.*

Cora was perfect. Weirdly perfect.

*So, those are a few things I'm looking for in someone and just a few things you can expect from me... Oh, I wanted to ask you... Have you ever looked at something so beautiful you felt yourself change all over? Or maybe you looked and saw and it saw you and you felt real, recognized? What was that thing?*

Every single time Josie answered the question the same, knowing Cora wouldn't hear her.

"You."

# Two Moons

The moon was the only thing that soothed Selene as a child. She was rambunctious, often crying and raging for what seemed like no reason, but immediately silent once under the glow of the moon.

"It was the only thing that made her quiet. Looking up at the moon, whether a sliver or the full round. Selene just had to have the moon shining down on her to rest. The thing calmed her so much I wished I could bring it inside the house." Her mother, Judith, would tell the story to anyone willing to listen, describing in detail how taking Selene's white bassinet out to the front yard was the only way she got a much needed rest from the fussy girl. The moment the moon touched little Selene she calmed and relaxed, drifting right to sleep.

When she was old enough, around fourteen, Selene took to sleeping outside in the gazebo every night. She'd drag her mother's old blue and gray sleeping bag out across the lawn, bunch it up in the corner of the structure and nestle in, craning her neck up at the sky.

Her mother didn't much mind. She was sure Selene would grow out of her "moon phase" after a time, much like Bobbi Donovan two houses down grew out of his obsessive love of dinosaurs and Genevieve from across the street grew out of her "pretty princess phase."

But Selene didn't grow out of it. Rather, she grew *into* it, feeling the heavy pull of the satellite more and more as she matured. The moon had a deep draw on her, more than other people who claimed to be affected by its ever-changing form.

Her desire to be near it, touch it, even kiss it made Selene crazy, sometimes irrational. She would look up, whispering to the moon, "I love you, I love you, I love you" with unexplainable tears in her eyes. When she stood in its light, warmth overtook her body and traveled so deep she felt excited and overwhelmed and everything all at once. There were no words or sounds she could make to explain what she felt, but Selene knew she was supposed to be up in the sky with her beloved moon.

* * *

It was quite possible the girl was special. The thought crossed her mother's mind from time to time. *Special.* It wasn't right that a child's obsession continued into adulthood. "Shouldn't she have grown out of this by now? Did I do this?" Judith asked herself, thinking of how she used to drag the bassinet out under the sky and allowed the girl to sleep in the gazebo night after night. Had she inadvertently exposed Selene to some sort of harmful moon rays that warped her? Was that even a thing? Judith didn't know, but she worried about her daughter. She was growing into such a beautiful woman, but this obsession made her a standout.

When Judith found Selene naked on the lawn the evening of her eighteenth birthday, she lost all hope that her daughter would ever be normal.

Selene stood in full view of the neighbors beneath the shimmering light humming *Blue Moon* to herself, her hands rubbing her oil-black skin while she sang and smiled at no one in particular and swayed left to right like a night lily in the breeze, wholly encompassed by her task.

"Selene, what are you doing?" Judith looked her daughter up and down, expecting to see some physical damage to explain her behavior. "Come inside, child. Put some clothes on this instant."

"Mother, I have to bathe in the moonlight," she babbled calmly. "I have to spread the moonlight over my skin. I want to smell like the moon. I want to be the moon. I am the moon. Can't you see? This is *love*." Selene continued to smooth her skin, massaging the moonlight like shea butter over her throat, pure bliss spreading across her face.

Judith knew there was no stopping Selene and no telling her that she was, in fact, *not* the moon.

Selene continued on, her behavior driven by a love of the moon and a desire to soak up as much moonlight as possible. Her mother did not pretend to understand, nor did anyone else in her life. She was, to them, strange, on her own planet, in a fantasy world where the moon simply loved her back.

But it was not a fantasy. The moon *did* love Selene.

Luna cherished her more than the night sky itself. From

the moment Luna rested her gaze on Selene as a child, she felt a protectiveness that had been reserved only for the stars. As the girl grew into a woman, her upward glances and whispered declarations of love made Luna desperate to know her, to be with her. Luna looked down on her human every night, plotting ways for them to be together and wondering if Selene truly meant it when she looked up at the night sky and said 'I love you.' Could she even know how much those sweet words and those wide brown eyes full of admiration focused up meant to a majestic moon? No one had ever shown such love and awe for Luna the way Selene had.

Luna watched for Selene all hours of the night and day, so much that she was often late or did not show at all in other parts of the world, leaving the night skies bleak and black. People began to think the world was ending, but for Luna the world was just beginning. Beginning to have meaning.

"Luna, you look all funny. What gives?"

Luna shot a glance over at Esme, her good friend, a star a few orbits away, then turned her gaze back to Selene. She had fallen asleep in her family's gazebo, like she used to do when she was a child. "Oh, it's nothing."

Esme spun around several times whipping purple gases around like a cape. She was a young star still marveled in her ability to fume. "I think it's that girl down on Earth. What's her name, Star or something?"

"Her name is Selene. She's gorgeous isn't she?" Luna's eyes glazed over with love. If only there was a way for her to swoop down lower for a closer look. But that was almost impossible. Any closer and she would surely disturb the tides.

"Yeah, she's pretty, Luna. But she's human. And she's

*waaaay* down there. And we're *waaaay* up here."

"I know, I know." Luna sighed. "But I just can't get enough of her. She's so, so…"

"Tiny?" Esme spun around until she was dizzy and let out a high-pitched laugh.

Luna chuckled at Esme's antics. She was supposed to be studying for her galaxy exam and Luna was supposed to be helping her. But Esme seemed more interested in spinning, and Luna was certainly more interested in watching Selene. If only she could absorb the dark-skinned woman's magnificence.

"I think I have a plan, Esme." Luna whispered so lowly her friend almost didn't hear.

"What do you mean? What kind of plan?" Esme skulked closer, her purple trail of gases fizzling out.

"I'm going to get her up here or me down there. I haven't quite figured it all out yet, but—"

"What?" Esme shrieked. "How do you plan to do that? If you get any closer you'll cause a tsunami or something, wreck the entire coast. You can't, Luna. You *can't*."

Luna heard what Esme was saying, but it didn't matter. She needed to be closer. She had to let Selene know that she heard her words, that she saw her dance, that *she* existed because of her. Luna changed the subject and pointed down around the gazebo. "Look at the moonflowers Selene planted a few days ago. They're my favorite. She knows my favorite flower, Esme. She loves me."

Luna eased her light over the paper-white flowers, touching them gently. Luna felt Esme's tight eyes on her, likely questioning her sanity. She ignored the glare.

"Luna." Esme was persistent. "You're, what? A few billion

years old? Do you really think she… I mean she's probably just infatuated, you know. A pagan or something."

*Some friend,* Luna thought, hitting Esme with a low blast of light to scramble her sense of direction. What did a silly star know? Esme slept all day and spent most of her time fuming out until she was in a daze, winking at airplanes she mistook for other stars.

Luna looked back down at the gazebo, but Selene was not inside. She was awake, standing in front of the structure with a handful of moonflowers. She reached them up toward the sky and smiled. Luna took a deep breath. Never had she felt anything so pure, so powerful and consuming as Selene's affection. Despite Esme, Luna knew. *This is love.*

Luna sighed, looking down. "Selene."

Selene was perfectly placed against the night, a glowing reflection of the moon, her gauzy, white gown flowing around her. She spun around, then kissed one of the flowers she held and offered it up to Luna.

"Oh, Selene. If we could just be together, the world would make much more sense."

Luna inched lower, reaching out to take the flower from Selene, but they were still much too far apart.

"Luna, don't," Esme warned.

"Shh…" Luna eased forward again.

"Luna, you're getting too close."

"It's fine, Esme. I know what I'm doing."

Luna had no idea what she was doing.

She wasn't sure if she'd explode or disintegrate or what, because anything could happen that close to Earth. The changes in the atmosphere, the tug of energy came on quickly.

But Luna couldn't stop herself. She kept moving, knowing she would soon be able to touch Selene, accept the flower she offered. *Just a little closer...*

Soon she was glowing and radiating light like she'd never felt before. A beam of platinum energy shot out in front of her, creating a path straight down on the ground where Selene stood.

The faint sound of Esme calling her tickled Luna's senses, but she didn't look back. She didn't want to see how far she'd strayed.

"I knew you'd come for me one day." Selene followed the path in front of her and stepped right up to Luna. "People think I'm crazy. But here you are, my love."

"Here I am." Luna didn't know what else to say. She was close enough to feel Selene's breath on her surface. She felt her core heating and cooling rapidly, expanding and shrinking until she felt out of breath and woozy. Her outer edge tingled with a painful pressure, but she couldn't force herself to pull away from Selene.

"Here." Selene reached out placing the moonflower on Luna's head.

The soft petals tickled Luna's surface. It was the most unexpected and exquisite sensation Luna had ever experienced, like what a shooting star must feel when bursting through clouds across the sky. Luna wanted more. She wanted to feel like that all the time. She smiled at Selene and blurted out the first thing that came to mind.

"Come back with me. Come live in the sky with me." She watched Selene's eyes grow wide as she contemplated the words. "You'll be the goddess of my sky."

"And you'll be mine," Selene said softly. She closed her eyes and nodded.

"You mean it?"

"Yes! I am the moon."

"We'll be two moons together."

Luna grinned and widened the path of platinum light, lifting Selene into her magnetic field. They rose from the ground and drifted slowly back into the sky, the wind billowing Selene's dress behind her like a banner. As they rose higher and higher, Luna memorized every dip and curve in Selene's face, realizing her smile was identical to a crater on her own dark side.

"I've always wanted to fly."

"You're definitely meant for the sky." Luna pulled Selene closer and twirled her around.

"More, more," she giggled, kicking her legs out against the air.

Luna did as she was asked, spinning and twirling Selene across the sky, watching as her smooth skin shimmered and sparkled with stardust.

"Kiss me, Luna. Don't let this be a dream."

A flutter of hesitation swirled inside Luna. She'd never kissed a human before. But, oh, how she wanted to now!

As Luna moved in closer, she caught a glimpse of Esme over Selene's shoulder, twinkling at her highest wattage. She gave Luna the thumbs up, then dimmed her light until she disappeared into the backdrop.

"A kiss under the moon means eternity, Selene. Is that what you want?"

Selene blinked her eyes and nodded. "Kiss me."

* * *

The bright light poured into Judith's bedroom window, waking her as it blanketed the room in a wide pattern. She rubbed her eyes and sighed with exasperation. *It's probably just someone using our driveway to turn around again.*

A quick flick of the mini blinds and the room would be dark again. Judith got out of bed, peeking through the miniblinds' slats out of habit. It wasn't a passerby turning around. It was the moon, beaming so loudly that Judith had to squint to continue looking at it. She knew she'd never seen the moon so large and white and... happy?

It seemed unnatural, a little scary even, and yet she was hypnotized. For the first time, she understood her daughter's love for the thing. It was truly majestic. "It's at least twice as big tonight," Judith mumbled, squinting against the light. She craned her neck closer to the window as her eyes adjusted. *Selene?*

"Oh, my God!" Judith burst out onto the lawn in the direction of the gazebo, hoping her tired old eyes were playing tricks on her. But she already knew that was Selene up in the sky, nestled close to the moon. She found the rumpled sleeping bag in the corner of the gazebo, and snapped her attention toward the sky again.

"Oh, Selene."

Judith tried to calm her breath as she watched on, but her heart thumped in her chest. She couldn't believe what she was seeing, and yet she knew it was perfect. The moon spun her daughter around on tiptoe until she was giggling and laughing, the sound ringing of pure joy.

A smile crept across Judith's face as the moon inched closer and closer to Selene. Their kiss shook the atmosphere around her, setting off a brilliant storm of shooting stars.

Her heart filled with love and sadness as she drifted back to the gazebo and sat down, finally calm. She needn't worry about her daughter being normal anymore. She was, indeed, special. Too special to be normal.

Judith blew a kiss up to her daughter. "Goodnight," she whispered and watched the sky transform and stretch to accommodate two moons.

# Meena & Ziya

Meena watched her lover bless the room. Her arms reaching up toward the ceiling as she prayed quickly to the four corners and smudged the air with the bundle of tightly wrapped sage. *Protection.* Ziya didn't have time for her normal blessing and candle lighting. The girl they'd come to see was fading fast, slipping in and out of consciousness. A bad heart made worse by tainted water.

The aunt called in a panic knowing Ziya might be the girl's last hope.

Ziya was the best healer, the most knowledgeable woman. She'd been tapped by the gift at an early age just as her mother had been and her mother's mother. Meena marveled at her healer woman's gift. She was drawn to it.

"Open the windows. Bring wet towels." Ziya placed her hands on the girl's forehead and cheeks. "My god she's burning up. We need to cool this child down." Ziya's voice stayed low and calm despite the urgency burning in her eyes. She was always so steady, careful not to bring more energy to a situation than was needed.

Meena helped the aunt open the windows. The cool evening air entered as if already aware of the situation, bringing its own powerful energy and healing medicine. Silver light shone down from the sky, anointing them.

"Welcome." Meena greeted the air and began helping with the wetting of towels. From the corner of her eye she watched Ziya begin to work. Her strong form kneeled down by the girl's bed. Meena heard her lover's knees creak as they touched down on the floor. *My old healer*, she thought continuing to watch her movements.

Ziya rolled the indigo dyed blanket down around the girl's waist and placed her strong hands on the girl's stomach letting the illness guide her hands to where the healing needed to happen.

"Ay, ay, ay." Ziya moaned in her throat. The girl's pain was seeping through. Meena recognized the deepening lines on Ziya's forehead. It was obvious Ziya could feel the sickness beneath the girl's skin. By the look on Ziya's face Meena knew this was a bad, unrelenting ugliness. Her normally smooth features wrinkled with sourness. Her thin brown cheeks puffed out as she energized herself for the work ahead. The thick poison festering in the girl's veins would make Ziya earn her title tonight, Healer Priestess.

"Meena," Ziya's voice was stern. "Bring me the salve from the bag. All of it."

Meena nodded thoughtfully and rushed for the jars of ointment they'd prepared just before leaving the house. Fresh was best. It was an old drawing salve Ziya's mother had passed down. Comfrey root, calendula flower, rosemary and a host of other powerful herbs from their garden went into the medicine. That was Meena's gift, making medicine from natural herbs.

She went toward Ziya with the two jars. She helped expose the girl's skin and began applying the salve. As they rubbed the girl down, Ziya's lips began to move with sacred words, healing words, prayers. Her voice grew louder, the words flowed faster until her head hung loose and the spirits came through her. Both Ziya and Meena worked the ointment into the girl's every pore until their fingers and hands ached.

Meena went to her bag again where she pulled a brownish orange stick from a soft protective piece of animal hide and lit the tip. The stick glowed in the dim room and began to smoke. She moved carefully toward Ziya, slowly blowing the tendrils of smoke toward her healer woman. More and more she blew the smoke, guiding it into Ziya's mouth until she saw her lover's eyes darken and the edges of her full lips curl up.

Ziya took deep breaths, pulling the smoke into her body careful to let none escape before it was time.

Meena stepped back to let Ziya work. It was always an experience watching Ziya heal the people of their community. Though sometimes it worried her to think that Ziya could one day die from healing another. That she could possibly take in the illness of a patient if not careful. Who would be there to heal Ziya? Could Meena step in to bring her back from the brink? Would her herb magic be potent enough? Would her love?

Ziya looked over at Meena as if aware of her thoughts. The intensity in her eyes answered Meena's question for her. *Yes. We are one, tied to each other, this earth.*

No matter the consequence Ziya was on this earth to heal.

To cleanse, to realign that which fell out of balance. Meena watched on as her thoughts roiled inside her. Ziya coaxed the smoke into the girl's ears and mouth and nose.

Within seconds the girl's back rose up off the bed her body arching and twitching. Her limbs dragged the sheets and she began to whimper and cry, her breathing fast and choppy.

"What's happening to her? Oh, my dear niece." The vocal aunt looked worried and frightened. She squeezed her arms as the color drained from her face like water from a pitcher.

Meena stepped in. This was also her gift. Comforting those who sought Ziya's help. She took the woman's hands and looked her in the eyes. "Ziya is drawing the poisons out. This won't be pleasant to watch, but I assure you, your niece will be well. Now we must let Ziya work." Meena lead the aunt out of the room and back toward the front of the house.

"Ziya is an old healer. She knows what to do." The reassuring smile Meena offered soothed the woman. But the girl's screaming followed by Ziya's hurried mutterings made the aunt jump. She wanted to run back to the room and intervene.

"I'm not sure about this. What if…"

"Tst, tst, tst," Meena's hand tightened around the lady's wrist. "She knows what she's doing. Have faith in your healer." Meena eased the woman back toward the sitting area and kneeled on the floor in front of her.

"You can trust and believe in that woman. I do. I know what she can do." Meena rolled up the sleeve of her blouse and held out her arm. A brown indention stood out against Meena's golden brown skin that traveled from her elbow down to her wrist. "She healed me. Ziya saved me."

The girl's aunt sucked in her breath. "What happened to your arm, girl?"

Meena closed her eyes traveling back in time while half listening for faint sounds from the back room should Ziya need her help.

"I had a wound that would not heal. No matter what I did. None of my herbal knowledge helped. No natural poultice or salve eased the swelling or the ache. I should have asked for help sooner, but I'm stubborn." Meena smiled, her eyes still closed as she remembered. "The infection came so quickly. It went straight to the bone."

More cries rose up from the back of the house followed by Ziya's calming voice. Meena and the aunt gripped each other's hands tighter and Meena continued.

"The pain was so bad I could hardly move. My vision blurred until I could not see. For two days I sweated as if rain was falling from inside me. I prayed. All I could do was pray."

"Yes." The girl's aunt squeezed Meena's hands.

"I prayed to the spirits, my ancestors. I called out their names one by one. Maria, Sousa-Linde, Jarol and so on."

"What happened, dear?"

Despite the pained screams floating from the back room, Meena smiled. "*She* happened. Ziya showed up at my door. The old ones heard my prayers and sent her to me. They sent me a healer. Ziya plied me with medicines, herbs from my own garden, elixirs and whatnot. And she conjured. Oh, how she conjured. Around my bed she walked a groove into the floor chanting and raising the energy needed to heal me. She pulled me right up out of my skin, separated me from the vile nastiness growing and swelling up inside me, then brought me back to earth and lay me down as gentle as a feather. She is a pure gentlewoman, a healer woman. She didn't leave my side for days."

Tears streamed down the old aunt's face. Whatever uncertainty she had about the healer was dissolved now. Meena's words were enough to make her see. To believe and have faith only made Ziya, Healer Priestess, stronger.

Meena listened to the woman's quiet sobbing and waited for a sign that Ziya had accomplished what needed to be done. She had a feeling it wouldn't be long now. The screams had quieted to low moans and whimpers.

Then all sounds stopped. Even the wind whipping through the window held its breath. There was no more whining from the back of the house and the old aunt only sat.

"She'll need rest. Lots of rest." Ziya appeared in the doorway leaning her exhausted body on the frame. Beads of sweat dotted her brow and upper lip. Her yellow shirtsleeves were rolled up high to the elbows. The salve left a sheen on her dark brown skin.

Meena noticed the veins in Ziya's neck and arms pulled tight. Her eyes were dull and watery.

"Ziya?" Meena rose from the floor and crossed over to her. She smoothed the wild hairs on Ziya's head and placed her hands on her shoulders.

"Shuh-sha. I'm fine." Ziya gave a weak smile, the exhaustion claiming her the longer she stood.

Meena had seen Ziya go to the end of the earth to bring someone back from the edge of death many times. But never had she looked so completely wrung out of herself.

"I'll get you home."

"I'm fine, I assure you," she said low enough that only Meena could hear and quickly grabbed up her hands for a loving squeeze. Ziya then turned to the aunt. "If the girl wakes in the night give her plenty of water. I've left herbs for you to feed her. The green ones on the first day she speaks, and the brown ones after that. She'll make a full recovery in two days, three at the most."

"Oh, thank you!" The woman began to weep. She clasped her hands together in front of her and gave thanks to the spirits. She brushed past Meena and Ziya then stopped to embrace Ziya in the circle of her arms. "Thank you," she whispered again.

Ziya stood in the doorway a long moment after the aunt released her. The healer closed her eyes and took in deep breaths. When she opened her eyes, Meena let out a shaky breath.

"This one took it out of me, Meena.

"Let's go."

For Ziya to say those words Meena knew some part of her must have been worried.

Ziya didn't argue or try to reassure Meena this time, only followed her out the door after gathering their things.

\* \* \*

Once back at their home, Meena began preparations for Ziya's grounding. Ziya needed to come back to herself, fully come back to this world. Meena saw the far away, distracted look in her eyes. She was still on the healing plane. Meena wanted her back as quickly as possible.

"You need to sweat," she said, helping Ziya strip off the

clothes she wore. Her knuckles brushed Ziya's breasts as she unbuttoned her blouse. Energy ran between them like electricity, Ziya's skin dimpled in response.

"I know you think I won't come back one day. From healing someone. But I will never leave you, Meena. I'll never be far."

Meena kneeled down, struggling to release Ziya of her skirts. She didn't know what to say, if she should say anything. It was true she feared that one day Ziya's gift would take her away. Tears blurred Meena's vision. She hated to even think about such things. She tugged the last articles of clothing from Ziya's body and wiped at her eyes before looking up at her. Beautiful. Goddess. Healer. Priestess. Lover. The words filled Meena's throat. Ziya's thick thighs twitched and her once smooth belly moved in and out with her breath, as she stood naked. Meena raked her fingers up Ziya's thighs toward her belly until her arms could stretch no more. She rested her forehead against her woman's stomach and perched her lips at the apex of Ziya's sex. Meena lingered there inhaling the pungent warmth of Ziya's essence.

"Sha-wei, my sweet. Come. Make me sweat, woman."

Meena rose to her feet with Ziya's help. Their arms tangled as they worked together to bring Meena to an equal state of undress. Fingertips lingered on soft curves. They shuffled to the back of the house where the rear-facing sauna stood erect. The small cedar box was built perfectly for the two of them.

Meena poured a ladle of water over the already warm rocks as well as a few drops of lavender oil. She felt Ziya's body hovering close behind her as she tended to the rocks.

"I heard you tell that girl's aunt I saved you." Ziya sat slowly, then turned to face Meena.

"You did. You know you did." Meena sat close enough that their arms touched. The feel of energy flowing back and forth between them was so strong, magnetic. Meena slipped her leg over Ziya's lap, unable to keep to herself.

The heat in the sauna softened and relaxed their bodies.

"Well, I think you saved me too."

Meena stared back into Ziya's face certain she had.

# Catch Me If You Can

The rain soaked dirt chilled Jaleesa's bare feet, mushing between her toes as she ran. Blades of grass licked at her heels, dew clung to her ankles, creeping up her muscled calves. The outside of her thighs grew damp the deeper she went into the forest, but she didn't stop.

"Yip, yip, yip," she chattered up at the sky. She transformed in a matter of steps. A wild thing under the moon calling out to her mate and to any creature within earshot. *Come on. Chase me. Chase me.*

Jaleesa was still two legged but with the most gorgeous, silky red-sunset colored fur all over. Her breasts and stomach took on a pale, opal colored fur that shimmered when she moved. She was double tailed. Each one twitching and testing the air. Jaleesa laughed out into the night, imagining what the two tails must look like, but not wanting to stop yet to see. Her body moved faster under its new skin, more natural than in the day. She was free and fluid as the fox in ways that she'd never be as a human.

"Yip, yip!"

Passing by the kudzu and nightshade she ran. Jaleesa cleared the yard in less than one hundred steps. She was in the woods behind her property in minutes. Leaves and small tree branches came in contact with her feet as she continued forward.

Jaleesa stretched her legs as far as they would go. She kept running. Her mind raced, passing back and forth from human to fox. Her vision grew sharper, more keen. Her nose flared sucking in subtle scents beneath the more obvious ones like ferns and pine and deer.

It had been three years since she'd gotten the itch to slip back into old skin. How she'd managed to stay human for so long surprised her. Jaleesa let out a loud cry. It felt good to be running in the night air like this.

How far behind Lomi was Jaleesa didn't know. She didn't look back over her shoulder either. Maybe she still stood in the doorway, refusing to give chase like she did sometimes.

"I have work in the morning, Jaleesa. I can't." Lomi's excuses didn't fool Jaleesa. She knew her better than anyone, she knew the truth. Shifting wasn't easy. It took a toll on their bodies. Sometimes the shift took too much energy. And there was always the possibility of getting stuck. Never being able to go back to their human form. Jaleesa never questioned it, though. How could she? She was part fox, part human. When she got the urge to shift she did. She couldn't deny that part of her.

Lomi was more sensitive about shifting than Jaleesa. She didn't like the pain of it, the tearing of skin, the ripping muscle, the displacement. Going back and forth messed with her head, left her feeling disembodied. Sometimes it took more than a day to recover. Jaleesa understood. She knew first hand what it felt like. The overwhelming heat, the surge and shift in hormones sometimes left her without full control. But it was who she was.

After running further than she ever had while switching over, Jaleesa slowed to catch her breath. She heard a rustling in the leaves over her shoulder and got her hopes up. *Lo?*

When she crouched and looked behind her she just saw a fat doe scurrying off.

Too bad it wasn't Lomi. She was a beautiful type of wild. Golden fur, blood-dark eyes. If she would commit to her shifts, it wouldn't be so bad, there wouldn't be so much pain and disjointed thought. Jaleesa learned that once she accepted what she was.

Jaleesa heard more rustling behind her while trying to decide if she was more attracted to Lomi's human side or the fox in her.

Maybe Lomi had decided to join her after all. She was certainly fast enough to catch up to Jaleesa if she wanted to.

Jaleesa sniffed the air for direction. There was certainly something there with her. The smell of heat, moving muscle, flesh and blood, made her body tense all over. *Not Lomi.*

Friend or foe? Jaleesa stopped and crouched. She eyed a tree, then leapt off the ground with all of her strength and power. She'd find out what lurked in her woods. Nothing was going to spoil her night out under the moon, howling like a Catahoula in heat.

Her claws dug into the tree bark as she gripped and climbed higher. She scanned intently searching for anything that moved or seemed out of place.

"Where are you little critter? Show yourself."

There! Her eyes spotted movement by the wet ferns. A mouse. Insignificant.

Jaleesa jumped down from the tree, still crouched low. She would run another few miles then turn back for home. Lomi would be in bed curled up like the perfect domestic housewife. It was cute how she tried to fit in. Hosting dinners, going to community watch meetings, going to bed early. Jaleesa wondered who it was Lomi was trying to convince that she was human. Other people or herself? Either way Jaleesa understood. Where they lived had changed. Houses were popping up daily; the city was moving further out in all directions. There was hardly anywhere for them to run anymore. They only had the acreage they did because a friend didn't want to see it sold to some commercial builder, so they cut a deal with Jaleesa. She took care of the land; it was part of her family.

Her fox brain kicked in. Something more substantial than a mouse was on her tail. Her instincts to run kicked up and she took off for the house. She only got three steps away from the tree when a shadow loomed over her and lunged in her direction. From the side she was hit and forced to the ground rolling.

Jaleesa growled and snapped at the attacker while trying to gain enough perspective to stand up right. She was pinned down though. The velvety black sky was peppered with diamonds and the silky grass crushed beneath her shoulder blades ignited her animal heart. This was part of it, part of what she craved and what she just couldn't get as a human. There was no equivalent. If she died tonight she'd be completely at peace with her choices.

The wet sloppy tongue slapping the sides of her face wasn't at all what she expected. A deep breath brought familiar fragrant scents into her mouth and nose. She relaxed beneath the assault.

"Yip, yip!"

Lomi didn't let up with the licks and kisses. She nipped the tender skin around Jaleesa's ears.

"I got lonely waiting for you to get back."

"You still surprise me, you know that?"

"Last one back to the house makes the bed in the morning."

Lomi hopped up and took off through the brush, leaving Jaleesa with only a fleeting glimpse of her white tipped tail.

Jaleesa jumped up and chased her. She would let Lomi win tonight. Her domestic fox had earned it.

# Harvest

Korinthia stepped out onto the porch barefoot in her blue floral housedress. The morning air hung flat and cool. A breeze would have been welcomed, but the lower temperature was a nice change from the recent month's dry heat.

It was early still. The sky was dark blue but lighter near the horizon where Maddie's house was visible just over the hill. Looking off in the distance at her nearest neighbor's roofline reminded Korinthia that she needed to take a bushel of mustard greens over. Maddie had been asking and asking about something to help get her bowels right again. Too much sugar and dairy in her diet had gotten her all kinds of backed up. Korinthia only came to that conclusion after talking to her. She'd take the greens over later on, but before it got too hot. The walk would be good for her. It would energize her spirit and perhaps wake up the little one. She patted the under curve of her high taut belly but stood still on the porch look-ing around.

Clusters of stars were glittering in the darkest part of the sky like rock salt. Things sure did look different these days. Different groupings of the stars had recently caught her eye making her wonder about what was going on up there. Korinthia thought it was a good sign whatever it was. When things changed up above it was sure to trickle down soon after.

Something scurrying on the ground by the row of carrots grabbed her attention. Probably a groundhog or rabbit looking for a snatch of something to eat. Korinthia didn't worry about trying to shoo it out of the garden. Everything with a mouth needed to be filled with good things from the earth. That's what her grandmother used to say. That's why she worked so hard to keep the garden going year round, full of nourishment and healing plants. People needed her green thumb to keep alive and stay healthy. There wasn't such a variety in vegetation for miles and miles. Neither was there anyone as knowledgeable about foods to grow and eat to fight off whatever ailments latched on to you. It made her proud to have such a luscious field of edibles that she could share with the people around her and use to heal and cure. The work she put into the garden wasn't just for the people she knew. It was for her too. Growing things kept her mind off the pain and heartache she'd been through. Three miscarriages and two stillborns in the last eight years left her feeling low. If she could keep herself from becoming pregnant she would. But it just always seemed to happen. Every few years or so, usually after harvest season. No warnings or signs or indications ever came to her either through her body or her thoughts.

It was as if the stories her grandmother used to tell echoed in her body's cells. "We got special gifts, us women. Sometimes our gifts and the gods get together, make an even bigger gift. Don't forsake it. Let live inside you the magic for such things." She'd wake up in the middle of the night feeling as if a small seed was sprouting deep within her. The nights when she realized she was carrying something new she would cry and cry and ask why this kept happening. She'd call out to her grandmother seeking answers. Her mind would race, wondering whether she'd be a mother this time. Or would it end the same as before?

Then as the months went by she would grow outward in her belly, feeling little kicks and swells of movement. She didn't know how to stop it from happening or if she could. But with each little kick she resigned herself to be a great mother. But after each unsuccessful pregnancy she would have an outstanding harvest, enough to share with whoever or whatever needed it far and wide.

Korinthia could have been the talk of the town as peculiar as her situation was. There was no man in her life, and no actual children ever appeared after any of her pregnancies. But her people didn't question what was happening to her or speak on it too much. Some years she would be big and round and some years she wouldn't be. Simple. When she was pregnant, Maddie would occasionally reach out and rub Korinthia's belly or put her arm around her and pull her close if they were walking from one house to the other. But she never questioned Korinthia as to whose baby she held inside of her. No one ever said anything negative. They all had a feeling it was tied into the great harvests Korinthia produced and perhaps speaking ill of what was going on with her might cause something to change all that.

Korinthia heard a few thumps and bumps out past where she couldn't see. She thought she heard a few mouthfuls of vegetables being dragged off past where she had the rutabagas boxed off. If what she saw and heard moving out there was an old rabbit, she didn't much mind. That swift-footed critter often helped turn the soil so she didn't have to.

Korinthia looked out over the garden again, longer this time. She was in a contemplative mood this morning, not ready to do too much bustling around. She pushed her gaze as far round the side of the house as she could see without having to twist her body. Everything was vibrant, green, and budding up through the dirt. Fat round cabbages and heads of cauliflower popped up nicely. She'd had much better luck with the zucchini and radishes this year. The zucchinis spilled into the rows waiting to be gathered and the radish leaves stood tall and full. Flowers were blooming just at the edge of her property and leaking sweet smells into the air too. White roses popped against the early morning darkness. Their green leaves laden in dewy sheen.

Korinthia moved toward the steps to start her routine of watering and weeding, but stopped. Her muscles twitched in her lower back and along her sides. She put her left hand out reaching for the unpainted wood rail and placed her right hand on her belly. There was movement. Just beneath her belly button, a spot she used to be able to see, but it was long since invisible to her eyes without the help of a mirror. The tremor shook her all over in a kind of slow motion. She could feel each muscle contract then release. Korinthia closed her eyes and took a deep breath. The inside of her mouth tasted sour. Nothing had moved inside of her for days. Was what she felt real or just some phantom kick she imagined? Thirty drops of cramp bark tincture for three days straight had settled her spasming womb and calmed the early contractions down to nothing, but now she didn't know if anything was still alive inside of her or not. She didn't want to think about birthing another dead baby and having to hike its body out past the glen into the woods.

Korinthia bent down slowly to grab the watering jug she'd left on the top step leading up to the house. It was half full from last night's rain and would make a refreshing morning to the plants in direct sun out front. She mapped out her day in her mind, shuffling feet across the yard. Water the plants, bring in the ripe tomatoes and zuccs, gather up some mustard greens to take to Maddie, and settle in to finish a few rows of the baby blanket she was making before she needed to start cooking.

Chills shimmied up the backs of her calves the further she moved toward the rows of vegetables. The dew on the grass tugged at her ankles and crawled upward till the hem of her old housedress was damp and clinging to her meaty thighs.

Shuffling her feet between the rows of squash and green beans, Korinthia moved without thought, taking special care to dampen the soil just enough, but not too much. The balance of air and sun and water had to be just right for things to grow. She'd learned how to take care of living, breathing things from an early age by her grandmother's side. Garden work and healing work taught her well about the cycles of life and growing things to maturity, keeping things healthy and whole. She looked down at the top of her belly. She'd been working extra hard to keep this one healthy and growing. There was another bounce of movement. Maybe she hadn't imagined anything. Maybe it would be all right.

She'd made it back to the side of the house where the dill and rosemary and hanging baskets of strawberries were awaiting their bath when the jug ran dry. The sun was just easing its way up into the sky as she turned the corner to refill the jug at the spigot. Another tremor of movement struck her on the left side of her belly then hit her again on the right. This time there was pain. Sharp, pinching spasms stretching across her belly and down into her legs that made her cry out. Korinthia forced air between her lips and braced both hands flat against the side of the house. From the corner of her eye she saw two brown and white rabbits hopping back and forth like they were in a dance. She shook her head.

Eight months seemed too far along for a loss. The furthest along she'd ever gotten was five or six months. This time would be more devastating than anything if she didn't get to keep the baby.

Her muscles went slack and saliva pooled in the corner of her mouth. She was going to pass out.

When she came to, Korinthia was lying on the ground. She looked straight up at the sky panting and trying to feel herself awake. Two large clouds as round as her belly were slowly moving overhead, blocking out bits of sun a few sections at a time. She felt wet and cold even though the sun was beating down on her, and sweat ran off her forehead down past her temples. The shake in her body dug in deep, back somewhere near her spine.

*This baby probably isn't going to come out alive either.* Korinthia instantly regretted thinking that. No good mother would shorten her child's chances by thinking something so ill. She closed her eyes feeling the clouds walk over her, casting shadow after shadow. Could she holler loud enough for Maddie to hear her and come up the hill?

She didn't notice the rabbits watching her until she tried to push herself up from the ground to sit upright. She was weak and only able to push up on her elbows before she had to take a rest and try again.

The rabbits were in a circle all around her. Looking at her, watching her every move. Almost as if they were watching *over* her. They held their circle, even when Korinthia was able to fully sit upright. She didn't know what was going on. There were at least forty rabbits around her. All just looking at her, holding her in this jagged, misshapen circle. She'd seen plenty of the critters roaming the garden, tasting the different vegetables, but never so many at once. She sat catching her breath and thinking about what happened. She remembered going over to the house to refill the water jug and then feeling sharp pain and getting light headed. There had been two rabbits hopping around like one was courting the other near the edge of her property coming toward her. She could have sworn there were only two rabbits.

Korinthia looked around. She was in the clearing behind the house going toward the woods. Had she crawled back there before passing out to get out of the sun's direct light? She looked at her knees and dress. She was no dirtier than when she'd been watering the beans.

One of the rabbits moved, scratched at its ear with a hind foot then continued to stare.

Korinthia placed a hand on her stomach. It moved in rippling waves like a thin membrane filled with just enough fluid. Her skin dimpled right on top like a fast moving current formed an air pocket underneath. She looked at her undulating stomach, scared to death that something horrible was going to happen. That she might die this time. She touched the dimple in the middle of her belly. It sank in a little then bounced back. Her eyes twitched back and forth between her belly and the rabbits who seemed to be moving closer, tightening the circle around her.

"This time is different."

Korinthia sucked in her scream and gasped. The rabbit directly in front of her, a deep dark brown one the color of tree bark, its eyes nearly invisible and with smooth ears, stood on its hind legs and moved closer. The other rabbits moved closer too, breaking the circle to come to her side.

The lead rabbit came to sit right at her knees. "I'm Jama. I have a message for you."

Korinthia tried to shrink away from the rabbit's voice. Its low, confident tone frightened her. Drops of sweat beaded between her shoulder blades. What message could a rabbit have to give her? Since when did rabbits speak a language she could understand? The moment she and Jama shared eye contact made her throat dry up before she could respond. Korinthia couldn't make herself move away from the rabbits. She reached for her belly, but two light brown rabbits were already soothing and petting her. They were murmuring tiny words against her stomach. Whatever they were saying calmed the rippling motion.

Korinthia looked at the rabbits surrounding her. They obviously didn't want to hurt her. They were in fact making her more comfortable. Several of them massaged her ankles and feet, drawing out the swollen aches she'd been experiencing.

Others played in her hair or rubbed her shoulders. She turned to Jama, waiting for the message.

Jama's lips parted, showing sharp upper teeth. A frightening smile if that was what Jama was doing, Korinthia thought, but she sat again waiting.

"Gangi is coming."

Before she could say anything, ask why she was being told that this Gangi was coming, Korinthia felt her womb growing hot. The rippling and rocking motion of her belly nearly thrust her flat on her back, but the rabbits helped her stay upright in the sitting position. She put both hands on her belly, feeling the warm and rolling waves taking over. This wasn't her baby. This wasn't the still child coming back after the doses of cramp bark tincture to quiet her premature contractions. This was something huge and life changing inside of her wanting to burst out.

"Gangi is coming," Jama repeated one last time then backed away. The rabbits huddled close around Korinthia. She could see their shiny teeth and their little pink tongues.

Tears seared her eyes. She had no idea what was happening, but the rabbits seemed to know. They understood the unnatural way her belly undulated and pulsed even if she didn't.

Korinthia's breathing increased as the pressure inside her threatened to push her in several different directions. She remembered the last time she felt her body pushing and pushing out the life it held inside. Maddie helped her deliver a baby boy as cold and as heavy as a rock. More tears stung her eyes like nettles. She thought about the other births and the spontaneous losses in the night. How she'd carried them to the forest wrapped in the knitted blankets she'd made for them. How she covered them in soil and put a seed or two of her favorite plant, amethyst, over their graves. She'd asked to be released of this responsibility. She wanted her freedom back, but that was not her destiny.

Korinthia looked to the rabbit closest to her. It was orange with wild tufts of hair growing up in every direction. It beat its foot against the ground several times in sucession, making dust rise.

"Your children grow in the forest. We watch over them." The rabbit playing in Korinthia's hair leaned down next to her ear to whisper to her.

"Thank you for allowing us to eat from your garden." Another rabbit, the one rubbing her shoulders, thanked Korinthia for the edibles. "You've helped so many of us, you know."

"We have always watched out for you in the same way you have watched over us."

The kind words distracted Korinthia from the tightening in her abdomen for a few moments. She hadn't really done anything. She just let the animals have what they needed from the garden. But she appreciated how kind and comforting they were being toward her. Especially now.

"Gangi is coming!" One of the rabbits started bouncing up and down. A few others started bouncing too.

Korinthia looked around to see if she saw Gangi, but nothing near the woods stirred at all in any direction. Not until a body seizing contraction hit her did she realize what the rabbits meant. Gangi wasn't just arriving; Gangi was being birthed. Korinthia was giving birth to it. Right now. In the woods behind her house. "I don't understand," she cried, leaning into a howl she couldn't contain. She cried and cried through the pain.

"Don't fight it. Breathe."

"The Goddess chose you."

The rabbits chattered all at once. It was hard to focus.

Korinthia sucked in air trying to keep control, but she was losing herself to wild thoughts. *Why did a goddess choose her? How did a goddess even know about her? What was this baby doing to her?*

The rabbits helped position Korinthia as her body shook from all the power coursing through her. They propped her up against lopped off tree stumps and rocks and whatever they could find. To cushion her lower back they gathered skeins of cool moss and fluffy fern tendrils.

Gangi was coming. Fast and with all the force of the universe.

Korinthia felt like she couldn't take it. She would be torn apart before she ever laid eyes on the baby. She flung her head back in agony and screamed.

The ground shook in waves beneath them, mimicking the rolling motion of Korinthia's belly. Plant roots rose to the surface like pulsing veins. Small puddles of water and thick green liquid bubbled up through the soil releasing a musky aroma into the air. The roots moved together, twisting around one another until they formed into one.

Korinthia watched with wide eyes as the main root head wriggled right up to her belly and latched on while the rest of it encircled her. She screamed, unable to control her fear. The rabbits had backed away leaving a path for Gangi and leaving

Korinthia disconnected from their soothing touch. The green liquid dripped from her pores like sweat and flowed into the ground as the root suckled from her stomach. Tears streaked her cheeks and she fought to get away from the cold roots pulling energy out of her. She felt like she was floating up, up into the sky. Her skin tingled like new cells were emerging all over her body. She threw her head back to look at the sun and sky as if simply looking away could take her out of the moment. Korinthia's womb flooded the root. Floral sprigs began sprouting on either side. Green, yellow-green, and brown sprouts stretched out transforming into squirming baby fingers, then hands, then arms. The thick bundle of ground root softened into flesh. A baby formed fully from the bundle of roots.

She was a mother. Finally.

Korinthia cried and cried, soaking her face and neck in salty brine. Her tears flew off her face in a gust of wind and rose up into the air until they reached the sun and began filling it with her love and relief and joy. The sun grew bigger and burned hotter than it ever had. Just as her last tears ascended, the sun shattered, causing night to come. Shards of stars rained down from the sky, landing on Korinthia's head and intertwining with her braided hair. Shiny strands of wispy silver grew along her temples.

Korinthia reached for her baby, the desire to hold her child close stronger and more urgent than anything she'd ever felt. But the baby quickly grew and grew until it was a fully formed woman. Disappointment shook Korinthia through and through.

The rabbits moved in closer again, all murmuring and chattering at once.

"Goddess is born. Gangi has returned. This is a blessed time."

Korinthia's eyes overflowed again. She looked at the being before her through blurry eyes, astounded.

As night settled in Gangi adjusted to her new state. She moved her limbs up and down and to the side. She practiced taking steps and walking until she felt comfortable enough to prance and spin around. She moved gracefully until a nice sheen covered her supple brown skin. Then she stood off to the side, taking deep breaths and sniffing every green thing she could pick up and hold and run her fingers across until she'd had her fill. She approached Korinthia, then stood at her feet.

She looked like a regular woman, young with bright eyes and full features. There was easiness to her, but knowledge too.

"Don't get up," Gangi said, as if Korinthia could rise at the moment. A bunch of rabbits scurried over to Gangi's side and let her pull from their fur. She spun tufts of their fluffy hairs between her palms, making herself a thin gown with which to cover up. She instructed the rabbits in a language Korinthia could not understand. They scampered off only to come back a few short minutes later with leaf pouches full of water they offered first to Korinthia and then to Gangi.

Korinthia was still speechless and fatigued from the ordeal of birthing a divine being. She let the rabbits continue taking care of her as she looked at Gangi and took in the gracefulness and strength and power that rolled off of her like fog down a mountain.

"First, let me say thank you for allowing me to invade your body." Her voice was a silky web of lightness. "I know that could not have been pleasant or easy. But you were the only one I could trust to carry me."

"Y-you… it was you in there this whole time?"

Korinthia hesitated to touch her slightly less swollen belly, but she finally placed her hands down. Her skin was warm and fragrant and vibrating.

"Not exactly. But for the most part." Gangi winked and created a breeze so fine and refreshing Korinthia and the rabbits sighed with contentment. "Secondly, I must apologize for all those false starts over the years. Reincarnating yourself is never easy. Coming back has to be done right. The timing has to be right, you see. I tried to compensate you in the best way I could. The harvests have been good to you, yes?" Another wink created another breeze.

Korinthia understood what Gangi just said. She'd been the one impregnating her, making her go through death after death all because the timing wasn't right. Korinthia's blood began to burn. The timing hadn't been right for her either, but did she get a say in being mystically impregnated time and time again? No! Korinthia gritted her teeth ready to let the goddess have a piece of her mind. But she stopped herself. The harvests had been wonderful for her people and for herself. There had been medicine because of those harvests. But still, it didn't seem fair for her.

"I know what you're thinking. And you're right. It's not enough." Gangi stalked closer after unwrapping the last of the leaf waters. She sat down on the cold ground beside Korinthia and grabbed both of her hands in her own. "Tell me, what can

I do?" Gangi looked deep into Korinthia's eyes trying to pluck the answer out of her head. But not all of Gangi's strength was ready to be used.

"I-I'm not sure."

"No? You don't want a child of your own?" Gangi moved her hands over Korinthia's belly ready to bless her with a child.

"No." As much as Korinthia wanted a child she didn't want to be pregnant again, not for another second. She covered her belly with her own hands blocking the goddess. She stared back at Gangi, intently searching for something in the divine's face and eyes. "Tell me what's happening up there." Korinthia pointed to the sky.

"What do you mean?"

Gangi's face softened even more and she appeared to have a current of energy racing under her skin. Her eyes lit up.

"Things are changing, right? The skyscape has shifted these last few years. The stars aren't in the same place anymore. And there are new stars, too. And you, why have you brought yourself back now? Why was the timing not right all those times before?"

Gangi looked distraught for a moment, like she had the weight of the world on her shoulders. "The world is changing. Even up there. And if we don't change with it, we won't be able to survive. I've created a world that is growing faster than I can handle. I don't think I can do it alone anymore. Will you help me?"

"How can I help you?"

A smile grew across Gangi's face and she laughed. "Well, if I am a divine being and you are my mother, you, now, are a goddess as well."

Korinthia let Gangi's words sink in. She understood.

"Thank you, again, for allowing me to be a part of you. I'll always be with you. The goddess is always with you, remember that." Gangi stood up, backing away from Korinthia. "I'm going to walk around for a bit. It's been so long since I've been this close to leaves and trees. It's intoxicating. Will you be all right to get back home? I can send for Maddie to meet you."

"I'll be fine." She was still thinking about what Gangi said about the world changing, about being a goddess. She watched her daughter walk toward the woods a few steps and all the rabbits, save a few that had nestled down to sleep, followed after her.

"Mother," called Gangi from a few feet away. "If you go into the forest tomorrow, there will be a surprise waiting for you." At that she disappeared into the dark woods. Korinthia listened until she could no longer hear the movement of the underbrush.

\* \* \*

Korinthia woke up at home in her bed the next morning. She wasn't sure how she'd gotten there, but she was sure Gangi and the rabbits had something to do with it. She sat up feeling changed. Not at all like she'd been sitting on the cold ground writhing in agony for a time until a being of light and wonder leapt from her body, but as if the world had shifted. She felt light and reenergized. Her muscles weren't sore at all, and she didn't ache the way she usually did after giving birth. She felt new. Korinthia whipped the covers back and found an almost smooth belly, hardly any sign of having been pregnant. She got out of bed to six rabbits spread out across the bedroom floor.

They each woke up one at a time and followed Korinthia onto the front porch.

"To the forest?" she asked looking down at the balls of fluff at her feet. They began to hop and jump up and down.

Korinthia had no set plan as to where she would walk. All the paths into the forest were mostly familiar to her anyway. She started straight back into the forest and followed the line of the sun. As she walked, white and yellow flowers began blooming at her feet. The rabbits stopped along the way to rub their little noses against the fragrant flowers then ran fast to catch up. The deeper they walked, the more things started to bloom and grow around them. Plants and flowers that didn't normally grow there along the hills and in the patchy shade sprouted with every step Korinthia and the rabbits took.

After a few miles of walking and enjoying the sudden blooms Korinthia stopped. They'd walked right to the spot where her last stillborn babies had been buried. Korinthia inhaled deeply as she looked up ahead. There were thousands of amethysts in bloom. Pale purple petals as far as the eye could see. Korinthia felt overwhelmed with the sense of sacrifice and knowledge. But she felt powerful and, for the first time in years, she felt free.

# What the Heart Wants

Saachi twirled herself around making her dress flare as she moved around the dinner table, filling it with plates full of juicy cuts of meat, spicy vegetables, and tender rice— all of Mona's favorites. She'd spent all day cooking and preparing intricate paper lanterns that she cut out and assembled by hand. How she adored doing special things for Mona. It was their one-year anniversary. Saachi wanted it to be memorable, so she planned everything with Mona in mind. Saachi even practiced word by word what she'd say to get Mona to move in with her.

"Darling, on our one-year anniversary, I propose we move in together so our love can bloom like the perfect flower." She'd said and done these things a few times before so the planning was not difficult. She felt this was her last chance to find the one. It seemed all her other friends were coupled. Some were getting married and others were even having children. It was embarrassing to not be at the same level as them. Mona hadn't moved in yet. Saachi knew she needed to hurry if she were to have what all of her friends had.

When Mona arrived she carried a bright smile and two presents under her arm for Saachi. "Did you cook all this? And decorate your house too? Wow, babe. Everything looks perfect." Mona kissed Saachi's cheek and hurriedly sat down at the table.

This was a great start. Saachi could see the appreciation on Mona's face. She was excited to ask Mona to move in and love her forever.

Without much ado they ate, talking in between bites. After finishing her second helping, Mona sat back in her chair licking sauce off her fingers and wiping at her mouth. "Mmm! You know spicy lamb and zucchini is my favorite. Saachi, babe, this was the best meal I've ever eaten. Amazing." She looked at Saachi with a glazed look. She was stuffed.

It was time to ask Mona the big question now that she was satisfied, relaxed and pliable. "I'm so glad you enjoyed it, sweetheart." Saachi placed her napkin on the table. "Imagine having this every night. You and me, delicious meals, cuddles, time together. Move in with me. Say you'll move in with me."

Mona belched abruptly. "Excuse me."

"I said I want you to move in with me."

"I heard you. I just don't know what to say."

"Say yes! We can live together and be with each other all the time. I'll cook for you and love you. We can get married and have babies and just be so in love. Say yes, baby. Move in with me."

"Whoa, whoa, Saachi, slow down." Mona pushed back from the table to give her belly and her feelings more room.

"Why? Why do I need to slow down? We love each other,

right? I love you. So much. And it's been a year. Why wait? It's been a year for us."

"Yeah, a year, Saachi. That's not a long time."

Saachi straightened her back. Heat struck her cheeks. "People get married after knowing each other a few days, months. How can you say a year isn't a long time?"

"Okay, yeah, in that context a year is longer than a few days or months, but…" Mona belched into her hand, again interrupting her thought process and giving Saachi time to cut in.

"What are you saying?"

"I don't know, babe—"

"What do you mean, you don't know? How can people know after a few months that they want to marry someone, but you don't know after a year?"

"Why are you so upset? I just don't think a year is enough time to consider moving in and marriage."

"You and a lot of other people!" Saachi didn't hold back.

"But, babe—"

"Don't 'babe' me! You don't love me! No one loves me! No one wants to move in with me or love me!" Clear snot oozed from Saachi's nose. Her gaping mouth leaked cries as her eyes watered. "Why won't anyone love me?"

"Saachi, what are you talking about?"

"No one loves me," she wailed. "I just want someone to love me."

"Don't you think you're overreacting? I do care about you, Saachi."

"But not enough to move in with me."

"I don't understand why we have to move so fast."

"That's what you all say. But you just can't admit that you don't love me."

Frustrated and confused, Mona sat stunned. Any attempt to comfort Saachi was brushed off. "Should I go, then?"

Saachi sat without saying a word. Her chest rose and fell with the quick in and out of her breath. Her heart was beating wildly. She wanted Mona to think about all she'd done, to say she was sorry, to change her mind. If Mona would decide to move in with her, they could forget this whole thing ever happened. But Mona had other ideas.

"If I leave, I doubt I'll come back."

Saachi still held her tongue. She knew exactly what was happening. Mona wanted her to back down, but she wouldn't. She would give Mona the silent treatment until she came to her senses.

"Saachi, I'm leaving. Don't think that I don't love you or care for you. But you're trying to force something that isn't right for me right now. If you think the only way someone can prove their love to you is by rushing a big decision like moving in, or getting married, then you don't really understand how love works."

Saachi watched Mona leave the kitchen, cross the living room, open the door, and walk out.

"She'll be back. This isn't over." Saachi sat back down at the table, dragging a fork through the uneaten rice. "Any minute she'll come back. She's the one. I know it. She'll be back." Time ticked away. Five minutes, then ten, half an hour.

The house felt cold and dark even though ample light shone from the fixtures and the thermostat hadn't moved.

Saachi moved from the dining room to the living room and sat in the middle of the floor with her legs folded under her. She fingered the hem of her floral skirt with one hand and gnawed on the other until she'd bitten off all her nails. She stared at the door biting at her lips and willing her lover to come back through the door.

"She has to come back. She is coming back," Saachi babbled to herself, nodding her head. A panic that, perhaps, Mona wasn't coming back beat at the base of Saachi's skull. "She has to come back or otherwise… I'll have failed at this again. Not again. Why do they all leave?"

The last bits of calm Saachi had been holding onto all dissipated. A screeching sound so severe it could peel wall paper clawed at her throat and tore at her until she was doubled over with her head against the floor. She beat the hardwood with her hands until she was weak and bruised about the wrists. Her sobs rattled the windows. Hadn't she been a good woman, an attentive lover, a creative cook, a great listener, a kind friend? Was what she asked for in return such a huge thing? Saachi didn't understand. Mona, Lindsay, Fabiola, Mia. All of them had reacted the same way when she asked them to move in, to love her the way she had loved them. As if she had asked them to loop a strand of gold around the sun. Impossible. How could they all reject her so? Was she so awful, so unlovable they couldn't bear to try?

Saachi gasped. The realization smacked her in the forehead. She was unlovable. Yes. The proof was right there. She was all alone with nobody to love her back.

The more she thought about it, the deeper the notion took hold.

Saachi sat on the floor rocking. "Unlovable, unlovable," she croaked out over and over again.

She screamed and lifted her hand over her breast. Her heart pounded steadily. Saachi tapped her palm over her heart, then bounced the tips of her fingers up and down several times.

"Yes," she said quietly, as if in a trance. "I know exactly what I should do." She then reached inside her chest using her fingers like tongs. She tugged once, then again. "Come out, you bad heart. You are going now. Bad heart. Such a bad heart."

Larger than most, and varying in shades of color not just red, Hudson, Saachi's heart, looked up at her from her hand, pulsing and pumping blood all down through her fingers. "Saachi, girl, you cannot command the heart to simply go. Put me back, dear, and we will grow closer and continue thriving."

"No. I don't think I can go on. I don't think I want to. There is no point. I am unlovable."

Hudson gasped and gushed in Saachi's hand dripping all over her skirt, seeping into the fabric and running all over the floor. "Not true, my dear. Not true at all."

"Look how broken you are, Hudson. How can you speak of growing and thriving and continuing?"

"I am not broken. That woman has only nicked a small part. I bleed to be renewed."

"And what about the others? They've hurt us too."

"Those were only nicks too, bruises if anything. We survived, dear."

"I just want what everyone else has, Hudson. Love. Someone to come home to. Babies. Is it all just a lie?"

"Patience, dear. Love, real and true, cannot be rushed. You cannot measure it by someone else's timetable."

"Oh, but it hurts so much, Hudson. I feel so alone." Saachi wailed unrestrained, her cries that of a wounded animal caught in some sharp, biting trap. She wished for a quick release or even quicker, death.

"Yes, it hurts. And it will for a while. But—"

"No! It won't hurt at all. Not if I leave you out and we go our separate ways. I don't need a heart anymore." Anger clung to Saachi's lips as she spit out words.

"But I need you. Put me back in your chest and sleep on it tonight. If in the morning you still want to be rid of me, I will take my belongings and leave you in peace."

Saachi sat alternating from sadness to anger while thinking about Hudson's offer. They had been together a very long time, he was her heart, yet she could only remember sadness and pain. It was pointless and tiresome to keep a broken heart when she was not lovable. She'd made up her mind. Hudson had to go. But because of the late hour she decided to put Hudson back in her chest for one more night before she sent him on his way.

"I'll help you pack in the morning."

"Very well, Saachi, my dear. Now place me back ever so gently so we may both get the rest we need."

Saachi lifted her tender throbbing heart and placed it back in her chest. She winced at the pain she felt as vessels and connective tissue rejoined. Hudson sighed with relief and pumped ferociously, sending blood to all the places that needed it. After re-establishing himself in Saachi's chest

Hudson started to sing, unobtrusively, the words to some made up song and hum a soft melody.

*"Believe that you are loved. That you are enough. Between your head and your heart you will feel right much. But you are loved, you are the universe, you are enough."*

Saachi exchanged her pretty floral dress for her dull gray pajamas, not paying much attention to Hudson's little song. She stood in front of the bathroom mirror examining her too small face and her big wide nose and her boring brown eyes. Slow tears rolled down her cheeks as she brushed her teeth.

"Why am I brushing my teeth or taking time to look in this mirror?" Saachi shook her head. "No one loves you and no one ever will."

All through the night her tears fell, but without so much as a break, Hudson kept singing the words to his song.

*"You are loved. You are enough. Between your head and heart you will feel right much. But you are loved in this universe. You are enough."*

Saachi woke up the next morning with a scratchy throat and itchy, dry eyes from all the crying, which only made her feel worse. She sat at the edge of the bed with her feet dangling above the round cotton rug she'd made out of old shredded t-shirts. Looking out the window, but not seeing the beautiful sun or hearing the happy birds' song. She did feel her heart pumping in her chest. She wondered if Hudson was awake. She hadn't changed her mind about letting him stay. After her sleep, she was more determined to send him away. She didn't want to feel anything at all ever again.

"Wake up, Hudson. Time to get moving."

Hudson just kept right on beating without a word.

"I guess we could have breakfast. A bit of coffee always perks me right up."

Saachi prepared the coffee along with toast and a scrambled egg, ignoring the elaborate dinner still on the table. The flies could have it. She didn't care. She sat at the dining table in silence looking at the chair where Mona had been sitting when she revealed her truth.

"How could you not have seen the truth?" Saachi asked herself. "You are pathetic. Unlovable in every way. Mona was right to leave."

Before Saachi could continue disparaging herself further, Hudson climbed up her throat, nearly choking her, and tumbled out of her mouth onto the table with a thud.

"Good morning, my lovely! Sorry about the entrance. These are for you." Hudson thrust a large bouquet of flowers at Saachi.

Coughing and gagging from the intrusion in her throat, Saachi needed a sip of water before she could take the flowers or say anything.

"Thanks, I guess." Saachi took the flowers, wanting to rub her face in them and inhale their intoxicating scent, but she held firm. She didn't love anything anymore, because unlovable people don't love anything.

"You guess? There are pink tulips, white roses, sunflowers, and even that one plant that looks like eucalyptus, but isn't. All of your favorite flowers in one beautiful bunch. Beautiful flowers for a beautiful, kind, *loveable* woman." Hudson smiled big then ran up one side of Saachi's arm and planted soft kisses on both of her cheeks and whispered in her ear. "Today will be better than yesterday."

She smelled the flowers then sighed. They did smell sweet and light like being outside right when Spring begins. But Saachi shook her head.

"Today can be many things, I don't care. I'm still unlovable and alone. I'll never be like my friends. No companionship, no children. Here, eat some egg and toast and drink some coffee. You must find a new home today." Saachi pushed the plate toward Hudson. She hadn't changed her mind about sending him away. With the flowers in hand she turned away from the table to look for a vase.

Hudson took his time with breakfast, chewing each bite of egg one hundred and forty seven times, each bite of toast two hundred times. Each sip of coffee took a full minute of careful swishing before swallowing so as not to burn his little mouth. And all the while he sang bits of the song from the previous night.

*"You are loved. You are enough. Between your head and heart you will feel right much. But you are loved in this universe and in the next. You are enough."*

Hudson took so long eating and drinking that Saachi had time to tidy up the kitchen and living room, take a shower, and put on her favorite green dress with the big pockets. She came back to the kitchen to get Hudson and take him wherever he wanted to go.

"Where shall I take you, friend?"

Hudson lay stretched out on the table rubbing his belly.

"Oh, dear, I'm not sure I can move just yet. That breakfast was divine. You are truly talented in the kitchen, Saachi."

"Thank you, though it was only toast and egg."

"Only toast and egg?" Hudson slapped the table. "That was a culinary feast. And your coffee making skills are a delight. Why, I've never had a cup of joe so smooth and rich before."

"You're such a kind heart. Thank you."

Hudson rubbed his belly again, then stretched and hopped off the table ignoring Saachi's question altogether.

Where are you going?"

"To sit on the porch in the sunshine."

"But—"

"Oh, it's best to sit in the sunshine after a delicious breakfast. It shows gratitude to the universe and gives the sun a purpose. Won't you join me?"

Saachi thought about it for a moment. She was eager to start her life without a heart, to be free of the hurt, but because it was their last day together she thought what could it trouble her to sit in the sun with him one more time.

"Sure, that does sound nice." Saachi followed Hudson out the back door to the porch and sat beside him on the wooden swing. Her backyard butted up against the woods. Many green things grew on the ground and attracted small furry animals. Saachi watched a groundhog pluck handfuls of yellow-green clover. Saachi laughed at the way its little mouth twitched up and down as it chewed.

"Isn't this fresh air wonderful? And look at those colorful

birds perched up in that tree, Saachi, aren't they beautiful?"

"Yes, they are. I'm glad you suggested sitting outside for a bit." They both closed their eyes while the sunshine warmed them from head to toe.

After the birds flew away and the groundhog moved on to another patch of greens, Saachi tried to motivate Hudson to tell her where he wanted to go start his new life.

"Are you ready now? It's been a few hours since breakfast. Have you gathered all of your belongings?"

"Not quite. I wish you weren't so eager to continue with our separation."

"Don't you see it will be better for the both of us? I won't be tempted to fall in love anymore or feel anything at all. If I don't feel, nothing will bother me and you won't bleed and hurt so terribly."

"Oh, I've already begun to heal, dear. You can't tell yet, but I have." Hudson crawled onto Saachi's lap and hugged her close.

"I'm glad you are healing, but you still must go. I want to be alone."

"If you insist. Will you help me gather my belongings?"

"Of course."

Hudson remained in Saachi's lap despite her attempt at standing. He lay stretched out with his legs crossed and his arms tucked behind his head. She had to carry him into the house. He made a comfortable nest out of her hands and laid back looking up at her with glowing tenderness.

"You are such a kind person. And you are oh, so loveable. Don't ever think otherwise no matter what anyone says."

Saachi wanted to believe her heart, but after Mona walked out she couldn't risk believing in anything or anyone again.

"What things do you need help with?"

"Hmm, well, I have some movies I need to get from that shelf over there." Hudson pointed to the shelf of dvds.

Lifting her hands up to the first shelf, Saachi placed Hudson on his feet. She watched as he pulled movie after movie off the shelf and handed them to her.

"It looks like you're taking all of them."

"Mmhm," he nodded.

"But, I really like some of these." Saachi looked at the cover art on *When Night is Falling* and read the back.

"Oh, but I *love* them. These are all my favorites. You won't be able to enjoy them once I'm gone anyway. You won't feel any connection to them."

"Oh, right, of course. Okay then. I'll get you a bag to carry them in."

Hudson continued pulling dvds off the shelf.

Saachi returned with a handful of grocery sacks for Hudson, but he was no longer on the shelf. He reclined on the couch with the remote aimed at the tv. He'd put a movie in.

"What do you think you're doing?"

"What's it look like? I'm checking out this movie."

"Shouldn't you be packing the rest of your things?"

"Oh, it won't take long. I know exactly where everything else is. Besides, I can't remember ever watching this one."

Saachi looked at the empty dvd case beside Hudson, but there was no cover art or words. "What movie is it?"

Hudson patted the cushion next to him. "Sit with me and find out."

He was delaying again, but Saachi was curious. She sat down and put her feet up on the coffee table.

The title credits rolled up the screen and music started

to play. *Listen To Your Heart, A Feel Good Movie* by Hudson scrolled across the screen. Saachi recognized images of herself smiling and laughing at every age. In the background Hudson sang, *"Believe that you are loved. I promise you are. Without a heart you won't get far. You are more loved than you know. You are enough. You are loved."* There were so many pictures and moments from Saachi's life, even a few from the future that showed how things would be if she didn't give her heart away.

The movie lasted for so long Saachi fell asleep on the couch. When she woke up Hudson was no longer beside her.

Saachi moved from room to room looking for her tender heart, but she didn't find him anywhere. His things were still there, which surprised Saachi. "He finally got the hint. I would've taken him to the train station, or wherever he wanted to go. Maybe he thought a clean break would be best." Saachi liked that idea. It was less messy this way. She took a deep breath, thankful for finally being left alone. She knew her heart meant well, but she knew what she wanted.

Saachi gathered all of Mona's leftover things and put them in a box for the city dump. She paid her light bill online, made a cup of lentil soup with cilantro and cumin, then settled into bed with a book that she wasn't actually interested in. She fell asleep so quickly she didn't hear Hudson singing his song ever so slightly in the background.

*"You are loved. You are enough. Between your head and heart you will feel right much. But you are loved in this universe and you are enough."*

Saachi woke up the next day without much energy. She felt drained and empty, out of sorts.

"Better than feeling sad and unlovable?" she asked her reflection. She didn't get an answer other than her own shoulders shrugging. Coffee would definitely help get her day started. She pulled her frizzy brown curls into a ponytail and splashed her face with water. "You are loved. You are enough," she sang under her breath while dabbing at her fresh face with a towel. Saachi moved toward the kitchen and the smell of coffee already brewing caught her nose's attention.

"Good morning, Saachi!"

Hudson moved around the countertop with ease. If his constantly pumping torso wasn't so messy, his movements would be adorable. But he was dripping on almost everything.

"Hudson, I thought you left already."

"I tried to, really, but the farther away from you I got the more and more I started to bleed out. I got woozy. I had to come back. I told you, I need you. I can't survive without you."

Hudson sat down at the edge of the counter. "I made you coffee and french toast."

"Thanks, I think." Saachi took the plate to the table, eyeing it intently. The french toast looked great, shiny and buttery with a dusting of powdered sugar all over it, but there was a giant red chunky glob in the center.

"That's strawberry compote not blood. I promise."

"Oh, thank goodness."

"Here's your coffee. I hope you like it."

"You didn't have to do all of this. I appreciate it, but really."

"There's more. Look under your placemat."

Saachi took a forkful of the french toast, which was perhaps the most delicious french toast she'd ever had, the corners were so crispy yet delicate and it was all covered in just the right amount of powdered sugar and strawberry compote. She quite liked that Hudson knew exactly how she liked her favorite food. From under the placemat, she pulled out a large handwritten card.

On it Hudson had written out in big bubble letters, YOU ARE LOVED. YOU ARE ENOUGH, SAACHI! YOU ARE BEAUTIFUL AND SMART AND WORTHY OF KINDNESS AND LOVE. The card was decorated with glitter and tiny cut out hearts and little hand drawn pictures of ice cream cones, and oddly shaped horses wearing fringed vests.

Saachi just stared at the card reading and re-reading the words and touching the pictures.

"I heard you crying in your sleep last night. That's why I came back. I know you said you wanted to be alone, but it didn't sit right with me knowing you were sad."

"I'm not sad," Saachi said with a tremble in her voice. She pushed the remainder of french toast around on the plate with her fork.

"Saachi, can I please stay? I'll heal quick, quick, quick and nurse us both back to our full selves. I can cook and clean and take you on long walks to clear your head. I'll bring you flowers and make you cards and laugh at all of your jokes. Just don't give up, okay?

"That sounds nice and all, but do you really think it's that simple?"

"Of course it is."

"But, how can that possibly be true?"

"Because you are loving and kind. Anyone who is loving and kind is lovable. Simple heart math. Loving plus kind equals lovable."

"I don't think it works that way."

"Yes, it does. Can you at least try it out again and see?"

Saachi slumped her shoulders. Her energy was draining the more Hudson tried to convince her. "I don't know. I'm not sure giving it a try is worth it."

Hudson paced back and forth on the counter top. He was dripping more and more with each step.

"Well, I don't know how else to convince you. Will you help me with something before you make your final decision?"

"Sure, what?"

"Well, this morning I bought twelve dozen eggs—"

"Twelve dozen eggs! What are you planning with that many eggs?"

Hudson grinned a big huge smile and rubbed his hands together. "Well, I love eggs. They're yummy."

"It'll take forever to eat that many eggs."

"Not if we take some and egg Mona's house!"

Saachi's eyes grew wide with shock and amusement. "We couldn't, could we?"

Hudson practically cackled when he jumped down from the counter. He scurried up onto the table and put both hands on his hips. "We most certainly could. And you can blame it on your broken heart." Hudson laughed deep from his belly, an ominous dark laugh and squirted blood into the air. "Whattaya say, Saachi? Are you in?"

Saachi looked at Hudson with new eyes. Her good, kind heart that brought her flowers, cooked her breakfast, made her a glittery card and a video was willing to be bad for her so she could feel good again. Saachi felt her energy slowly coming back. She'd never egged anyone's house before. She'd never torn herself up over a woman's rejection either. There seemed to be a first time for everything. Saachi stood up from the table and grinned back at her shiny, bleeding heart.

"If it's what you want. We can go egg Mona's house." Saachi tried to hide her smile.

"The heart wants what the heart wants!"

# Life Cycle

Khalida walked slowly down the hall. The smell of antiseptic and industrial grade cleaner made her stomach churn, but hospitals were a part of the job. She'd arrived early to observe and get a sneak peek at the newborn babies before collecting at midnight. Something about the babies all bundled up, unaware of the life that would take hold of them and either make or break them made her hope again, feel a little bit like she once did. Human and alive. Sometimes a baby even caught her eye and smiled, reflexively, before drifting off to sleep.

Tonight on her way to the nursery she got a strange feeling. A tingling sensation that tore up and down her spine. Something buzzed in the air that made her look around. So much death and transition everywhere. It could be anything really.

She sensed a colleague down the hall gathering what was left of a horrific car accident. Two children in the vehicle were thrown from the car. They died on impact. The grandmother, who was riding in the front passenger seat, arrested twice on the way to the hospital. Medics couldn't get her back after the second time her heart stopped. And the mother— who was driving her children and mother-in-law to the movies while trying to text her husband— wouldn't make it through the night. A shard of metal from the sign she hit sliced into a main artery. But they were all clinging on to each other making it difficult for Death to do his job. They were all screaming and pleading with whom and whatever they thought could change the outcome. Khalida understood their urge to cling to whatever remnants of life remained. But it was pointless. A wave of their collective sadness and anger washed over Khalida and she reached out to her colleague.

*Death, do you need assistance?*

Khalida made the connection easily, ready to step in and help. She was familiar with the reluctance of letting go.

*This is a rough one. I think I've got it under control though.*

*I'm available if you change your mind. Families… they can put up quite a fight.*

Khalida disconnected, but still sensed something else, something closer, more than life transitioning.

The heavy pull of whatever was taking place in the hospital made her long for the days of unknowing. Before becoming Khalida— immortal and deathless— she was just Khalida, a woman. A woman who enjoyed warm spring days, mint gelato and sleeping in. Reading suspense novels and snuggling on the couch with Celia, her partner, lover, friend. Before she knew the intimate details of death, Khalida didn't give it much thought. Dying was a part of life that she'd much rather deal with when she was dead.

But Celia got sick, terminal. A rare autoimmune disease doctors knew very little about took Celia from the energetic, spontaneous woman she used to be to a weak shell of herself. Losing Celia became a permanent fixture in the back of Khalida's mind and death became all she could think about. Day and night. She sat by Celia's hospital bed, holding her hand and keeping watch, keeping death away for as long as she could with the sheer force of her love. When Death came she'd be ready. She'd be there to turn him around. *Go away. You can't have her.*

But that was not how it went. Death did come. Nothing at all what Khalida expected. He was not a grotesque, menacing figure. He wasn't greedily snatching for Celia. He looked peaceful, helpful even. Soft understanding eyes and a sympathetic smile filled his entire face. He'd been there with them all along. He wasn't going away. At least not without Celia.

Death took his place by the bed and looked Celia in the eyes. He saw how tired she was. She was ready and had accepted what was going to happen with much more grace than Khalida had.

She held tight to Celia's hand. Tears flooding her eyes and fear taking up space in her throat until she could squeak only a few words. "Don't take her."

"This doesn't have to be the end, Khal." Death's response came in a soft musical tone. Celia's voice. That only made Khalida cry harder and try to hold on tighter.

"Ceels, please don't leave me. We can keep fighting this. Please don't go, baby."

"Oh, sweetheart," she said, her breath labored. "I have to. This body can't take much more. I'm wrecked. My spirit needs a rest, Khal." Celia with Death's strength stroked the back of

Khalida's hand, then her cheek. It was a gentle, loving farewell. "You can finally stop pretending that you enjoy my cooking," she quipped.

Khalida choked on tears and abrupt laughter. That was her Celia. Easily able to make her laugh and want to smile in the toughest situation. How was she supposed to go on without that in her life? Khalida placed a kiss on Celia's temple right near the crescent moon birthmark no amount of makeup could cover up. She was desperate for a solution. There was no life without this woman beside her. There would be no more laughter for her. What was the point of finding love, real love, if it didn't last? If it was just shortly balanced between life and death. Khalida's sadness turned to anger so quickly she didn't quite recognize it.

"No!"

Khalida took her hand from Celia's, roughly swiping at her tear stained face. She shook her head not accepting any of this. Khalida looked Death in the eyes. "Take me instead. I don't have a life without her. I might as well be dead."

"Khalida! No!"

"What choice do I have, Celia?"

"The choice to live. To remember me, honor what we had." Celia struggled to speak. She was fading quickly with Death at her side. "Besides, what kind of life would I have if you're not here?"

Death stood quietly except to relay Celia's words until the back and forth between the women became nothing more than selfless pleas to let the other one go.

"Khalida, I'm sorry. I can't exchange your life for hers. It doesn't work that way. Celia is obviously ready to leave this

Earth and I must abide by the rules of life and death. But," he said, shifting his eyes between the two them, his voice never rising above a soft purr. "I can facilitate a way for you two to be together in another capacity later on."

"What does that mean?"

"Yes!"

Khalida didn't think twice about being with Celia no matter the circumstances. Making a deal with Death seemed the least of her concerns. She just wanted Celia.

Celia of course wanted details. She never just went unknowingly into anything.

"Khalida, you would be under my service for a time. Essentially halting your human existence— you wouldn't die per say. But most earthly experiences would no longer be at your disposal."

"And when would I get Celia back?"

"Celia," he said, turning to her. "You would return in a cycle of rebirth— human of course— once your spirit has had a nice rest."

"We'll do it!"

"I don't know…"

"Celia? He can make it so we are together again. I want that. I'll always want that. I'll always want you."

Khalida witnessed Celia's reluctance. She could understand Celia's hesitation. One life with all its ups and downs was difficult enough. She'd been in the same hospital room for months. Death probably did sound like a nice change from the pain she was experiencing, her nervous system attacking itself and slowly leaving her hollow. But how could she deny the woman she loved a chance to be together again?

Khalida was willing to swap her life for Celia's, no questions asked. The outcome would be worth any amount of service Khalida had to provide. She didn't care what she had to do.

Khalida took Celia's hands in hers. "This is the only way. Please, Celia. I don't want to live without you."

\* \* \*

Khalida found her way to the birthing suites. Her mind had wandered back ten years though her feet had propelled her forward. She tried not to think of Celia and the time that had passed. It had been a mistake to bargain with Death. That she now understood. But back then, staring down the thought of losing Celia forever had been the one thing Khalida couldn't bear. Her desperation and fear of being alone had driven her. She should have listened to Celia. She should have let Celia go and grieved properly.

Instead, she agreed to serve under Death with the hopes of one day crossing paths with Celia again. So far during the ten years time that had past Khalida had only taken lives, guided people to their final resting destination and lost all sense of herself. She was beginning to feel as though she would never again see the woman she loved.

Khalida followed the curve of the hallway and stopped just outside of room 1010. There were several births taking place on the hall, but the energy pulsating around this room made her stop. The births and visits to the nursery were the only things that truly made her feel anything now. She eased into the room unnoticed and stood behind the doctor and assisting nurse.

All at once the comfortable warmth that had surrounded the baby for nine months was gone. She was being thrust down and out, away from the safety and warmth of her mother's body. Sounds all reached the baby at the same time. Monitors beeping, people talking to and instructing each other. Everything assaulted the little one's ears, eyes, and skin all at once. A slew of signals bombarded the baby's brain like the switch to a complex machine had been flipped and then she was breathing, kicking, screaming, blinking, reaching, shivering.

The weight of her first full breath smothered her. The air inside her lungs didn't feel smooth and liquid-warm anymore. It was cold, heavy, metallic. The sobs escaped her mouth before she could rationalize what was happening. The sound of her own voice making shrill vibrating squeals frightened her until all she could do in response was scream and cry more.

Between blinking lashes she caught glimpses of a figure standing separate from everyone else. The baby focused on the deep maroon cloak covering much of the entity until her eyes fully adjusted. *There. I can see.*

The others in the room all reached for her in a choreographed series of movements, cleaning her off with soft warm rags absent of scent. Their hands worked fast to clear the glop from her nose and mouth. They tested her reflexes, checked her temperature, measured her from tip to toe, and weighed her. Through all of that her eyes never strayed from the figure standing apart from the others. There was something extremely familiar about her. Her eyes were slightly shadowed by the oversized hood of her deep maroon robe. But her earth brown skin absorbed energy, like she was under a spotlight.

Her lips stretched wide in a lifeless smile, as if she were trying to remember how to use her mouth to express emotion. Her long arms wrapped around her torso, a gesture that looked more like a reminder to not touch than a comforting hug. Everything about her was recognizable, yet new.

The baby didn't know how that was possible, her being brand new to the world, but it was. She felt an inescapable desire to call out to the figure. *Who are you? Do I know you?* She wanted to scream out, get the figure's attention. But she didn't yet have control of her tongue or speech.

Hands reached for the baby, wrapping her in rectangular softness that edged off the chill on her skin. Her attention was drawn to the doctor's finger wagging back and forth in front of her. She followed it with her eyes before yawning and testing the function of her hands and arms. When she looked up again the maroon clad figure was gone. A heavy sinking feeling washed over the newborn.

"She's alert and very responsive." The doctor carried on with her assessment, assuring the parents their little girl was healthy and well.

"What is that mark near her eye? A bruise?"

"No. A bit of hyper-pigmentation. A birthmark. A crescent moon looks like."

"I'll mark it on her chart, Dr. Wynn."

"Congratulations, parents! Do you have a name?"

"Jasmine. Her name is Jasmine."

The baby started crying again. *My name is Celia! I'm Celia.*

# Me, the Moon, and Olivia

"There is a woman living on the moon."

I say this with all seriousness. I'm looking out the window of my therapist's office. Her lawn needs some TLC. The grass is a sickly yellow-brown color and the shrubs all look like someone tried to shape them into animals but got tired and gave up. There's an elephant missing its trunk and a way too skinny buffalo right outside her window. "There's a woman living on the moon. I've seen her," I continue. "She's black like us. Sometimes her hair is straight, but mostly she wears two giant Afro puffs and a crown of neon flowers. She has a patch over one eye."

I turn from the window and look at Olivia. Dr. Olivia Michelle Greyden. She tells me to call her Olivia. Selling that doctorate short if you ask me. I'd milk it. Doctor everything. Stationary, license plate, coffee mugs. Hell, you can get your name printed on just about anything these days. People would see me coming. Dr. Nideana Joy. Ha! Dr. Joy. Well, I should work on that right away. Everyone needs joy in their life.

Olivia isn't paying me the slightest bit of attention. She's staring down at the notepad in her lap. There are three dots in the upper right hand corner. She's connected two of them with a single line. The last has two thick lines connecting it to the other two and she's enclosed those dots in a circle. Squiggly lines rain down like detached tentacles. She doodles when she's thinking. I don't know what it all means. Maybe she's thinking about Liam. *Liam-Liam-Bo-biam-Banana-nana-Fo-fiam.* Liam's her boo, boo-thang, her man, the fiancé. Well, he was her man. He was arrested last week. Fraud. He got his hands on the confidential information of two high-profile patients and tried to sell their names and stuff. It's in three of the local newspapers. Olivia's name was even splashed across the television on the evening news. I don't like the news. It makes my head hurt and my stomach sick. Just like when I get too hot or have too much caffeine. There's never any good news. People are so mean to each other. It's always bad news. All the talk about Liam will die down in a couple weeks, I'm sure. I hope. Olivia isn't looking very good right now. The picture of Liam isn't on her desk. I wonder if she knows I know. She knows. Everyone knows. Some people are saying she was complicit.

C-o-m-p-l-i-c-i-t. That she knew what he was doing and that she helped him. They say she only turned him in to stay out of prison.

I sigh out loud, really loud. It gets her attention. She looks up from the notepad.

"I used to look up at the moon," she says. Not what I expected her to say. She's been listening the whole time. "When I was a little girl I used to look for the face, the man on the moon. Maybe it was a woman this entire time." Her smile is a straight line pulled up at the edges by invisible string.

"You're not going to tell me there's no woman living on the moon? That I'm avoiding my real issues?"

"No," she says. "I've learned that pretending not to see what is right in front of us is just as troublesome as seeing it. What's right in front of us is often the truth." I don't think she's really talking about the woman on the moon. She's talking about her Liam. Olivia uncrosses her legs and re-crosses them in the other direction, right over left. Her skirt is strained across her knee; the thread at the hem unravels a little bit and puffs up. Will it unravel all the way if she moves again? Now I'm concerned... not concerned, just interested. I had a pant leg do that once. Just an inch of thread came undone and by the end of the day my entire pant leg had unraveled and the hem fell out completely. I got it caught on everything during my shift at the dish factory.

"Olivia, are you all right? You seem different today."

I hope she doesn't mind me asking. I know I'm the patient, but she really isn't looking so good. Her usual reddish-brown skin is flat out ashy. There's no light behind her eyes. Her hair is pulled in a messy bun. Unruly dreads reach out in the back waving like fingers. She doesn't sound like herself either. Her voice sounds far off, flat like she's in a tunnel, she's breaking up. *Shhh, shhh.* I kind of like this different sounding Olivia. She sounds like me. But if she's not the voice of reason in the room, then that means I have to be, right? Dr. Joy is on duty.

Olivia looks at me. Then after a moment of deep eyeballing she lets out a snort, then another one and that one brings an entire line of snorts until she is full on laughing. I'm laughing now too. I don't know what about. We sound like two old friends giggling about something that really isn't all that funny, but caught us completely off guard. Our laughter settles just above the Berber carpet and waits should we need to kick it up again.

"Liam, my fiancé, ex-fiancé, is in jail."

I loosen my mouth in faux surprise and let it hang open.

"I had to turn him in or risk losing all this," she says pointing toward the room. She places four of her fingers on her chin. "I suspected," she continues, shaking her head. Her eyes are glassy, shiny enough to ice skate on, but she doesn't cry. Not even that silent crying that I've gotten so good at when my head is pounding and I see green clouds behind my eyelids. Not nary a tear on her cheeks. Do therapists cry?

I open my mouth to ask what she'll do next, but she stops me with a raised palm. Don't. Stop. Wait, her signal goes.

"This is inappropriate of me. I apologize."

"I asked. It's okay." I'm truly interested.

"Still… this is your time," she says, going all profesh on me. She's always so put together. I want to be like that, put together, cool in a crisis. But since I got hurt my head goes all old-school dial up sometimes, lots of noise and static, but no connection. I have trouble remembering things. I see things I shouldn't see. It all makes me feel bad about myself. I have to admit, though, I like the idea of Olivia unraveling a bit. That brief moment of her laughing out of control and dishing about Liam made us equals. Sort of.

"Tell me about your woman on the moon," she says, and I do. I tell her everything I can remember.

* * *

Two weeks later when it's time for my next session with Olivia I arrive at her office like I always do. I'm six minutes early. Ronnie the receptionist is in the break room. I can hear her clearing her throat and microwaving something. Probably tea. She likes tea. She'll be right with me. That's what she'll say when she comes back to the front.

The waiting area is cozy. Warm colors. Creamy yellow walls that melt like butter if you stare at one spot too long. The lights are soft and run all the way across the ceiling like train tracks back and forth. I like that, I like the extra fluffy chairs too. I always try to snag the sunset orange chair by Ronnie's desk. It's like sitting inside a dreamsicle. You can see the main entrance and the hallway to the bathroom from there and the magazines on the end table are the newest.

When Ronnie comes out she looks surprised to see me. She should be used to me being early by now, but she's a weird one too. I think Olivia gives her a discount on therapy.

"Nideana, what are you doing here?"

"It's Thursday, right?" Sometimes I do get my days mixed up. I look down at my watch to save us both any embarrassment, but I'm right on. It's Thursday, twenty-five after four. "I'm here to see Oli—, Dr. Greyden."

"She canceled all her appointments this week. You should've gotten a message on Monday."

Even though I delete all voicemails without listening to them, I shake my head. The idea of someone's voice trapped in a digital prison seriously freaks me out. How can their voice be in the machine and in their throat at the same time? How?

"Did she say when she'd be back?"

"No, but she rescheduled you with Dr. Greg Lumus for next week. He's great. You'll like him." Ronnie pulls a card from her desk and extends it to me.

I look down at the card and read this new doctor's name to myself. L-U-M-U-S. The *s* slithers toward the corner and I shut my eyes. When I open them again it's back, just sitting there. For a minute or more I stare at the card. I can feel one of my vision headaches pressing down on my right eye. When I look away from the card I see Ronnie staring at me. I smile and say thank you.

I leave when Ronnie excuses herself to the restroom. I don't want to see Dr. Lumus with the moving *s*. I want to see Olivia. I can wait. Yeah, I'll just wait until she gets back. She is coming back. She sent her fiancé to jail so she doesn't lose her practice. She won't blow off her patients to be with a thief. Unless she is a thief too. But I don't think she is. She was a woman inside of a therapist.

On the bus ride home I started to think about what Olivia would say to me when I got really agitated and frustrated. "Take some time," she would say. "Breathe. Make your lists and read over them." Simple, but it always worked. Maybe she was taking her own advice. That made sense. Taking some time to sort things out so she could come back stronger and better. Maybe she was making a list of all the ways she was special and reading them out loud. Next time I see her I'll ask if that's what she was doing. I bet she'll say, "Now, Nideana, we are here to discuss you," and be all profesh and stuff. But I'll know that's what she was doing.

"Taking time is mighty fine," I sang from the bus stop around the corner from my apartment. "Taking time is mighty fine. I do it all the time." I thought my jingle was phenomenal and made a mental note to write it down when I got inside. I would probably forget. When I unlocked the screen door something over my shoulder caught my attention. The moon was out even though it was still early in the evening. It was all white and cloudy and glowing. I decided I'd make dinner and sit out on the porch. Maybe I'd get a glimpse of my woman living on the moon. She really was there. I've seen her several times. When I talked to Olivia about her she seemed interested in hearing more about her, what I thought seeing her meant.

"Who do you think it is?" she asked me.

I shrugged. "I'm not sure. Maybe she's like a protector, a watcher keeping things from getting out of hand."

"Someone to watch over you?"

"And you too, Olivia. At that vantage point she's likely able to see more than just me."

I think she liked the idea of that because she smiled and put the notepad on her desk.

I dropped my broccoli salad on the floor. I was able to save the edamame, so I sprinkled them on top of my Thai style noodles and went outside with a glass of ginger ale.

The moon had drifted higher in the sky. Those craters would make a perfect wormhole. I thought about the *s* on Dr. Lumus' business card wriggling in and out of those holes, burrowing in and snacking on the crumbs inside. It was a silly thought. If there were crumbs they would have fallen out by now because there's no gravity, right? Unless the woman living there ate them for dinner.

My phone rang just as I settled into the idea of the woman snacking on the moon crumbs. "Hello, hello," I answered on the second ring. I didn't want anyone being sent to voicemail.

"Nideana, it's Dr. Greyden, Olivia."

"Hi, Olivia!" I tried to hold in my excitement, but I was glad to hear from her. "Ronnie said you left a message about cancelling appointments, but I didn't get it cause I delete all my voicemails, but I told her I never got it at all and I shouldn't have lied."

"It's all right. I wanted to call to apologize. I shouldn't have canceled on you. I should have remembered that you don't take messages and there might be confusion if you showed up at the office."

"It's okay. I'm okay. You have to take some time away to think and stuff."

"Yeah. I do. But you should see Dr. Lumus. He's very good. He'll listen to you."

"I don't know. The *s* in his name has a mind of its own. I can wait for you to come back."

"Will you at least think about seeing Dr. Lumus?"

I paused for a long time. I don't want to commit to seeing someone new. "I'll think about it." I tell Olivia I'll think about it, but I'm not going to. Not really.

"Good." She sounded like she was smiling, but not all the way smiling. Just one corner of her mouth, maybe. There was something else there blocking her full smile. "I went to see Liam," she said in a low tone and I understood the something else. "I drove all the way to the jail. I got inside and… I couldn't. I turned around and left."

I didn't know what to say so I just listened.

"I still love him, Nideana." Her voice was hushed like she was sharing a secret no one else should hear. "I know I shouldn't, but it's like someone hit me in the head and everything is rattling around not making sense. I'm a fool."

"Am I a fool too?"

"What?" Her voice was still hushed and smooth.

"Well, Sometimes nothin' in my head makes sense. My accident. I was hit in the head, remember? A stack of dishes fell on my head at the factory and cracked in half. Cracked me open."

"Oh, Nideana, I'm sorry. I shouldn't have said that."

"Am I a fool?" I shut my eyes tight. A buzz sounded deep in my ear. I wished I'd sent Olivia to voicemail, to the voice wasteland. I didn't feel good.

"No, of course not. I just meant that I'm all mixed up."

"Do you cry, Olivia? Do therapists cry?"

"Yes. Of course I cry. Therapists cry. Some of us even have our own therapists."

"Oh. You guys must be really messed up after listening to patients all day. Do you talk about me to a therapist?"

"Hey, are you looking at the moon tonight?" Her quick change of subject turned my heavy mind over. I wanted to know what she talked about with a therapist. Wait, was I her therapist? I thought about that for too long, then remembered she'd asked me a question.

"Yeah. I'm outside with a ginger ale. Why?"

"I am too. I'm sitting on my balcony looking for our woman who lives on the moon. Do you see her tonight?"

*Our woman?* "No, not yet."

"Do you think she'll show up?"

"Maybe. I don't know."

"I've started looking for the moon every night. Thinking and wondering what it would be like to be up there looking down on everyone and everything."

"Uh-huh," I say into the phone. I've stopped concentrating on the sound of Olivia's voice. Dust and crumbs started falling from one of the craters on the moon and formed a sort of cyclone on its way down to the ground. "Olivia I have to go now."

"Is everything all right, Nideana? You sound…"

"I have to go."

My moon woman was tunneling toward me. I didn't tell Olivia that I saw her, but my gasp must have alerted her that something was wrong. I dropped the phone and stood up, pressed my back against the side of my building. Olivia still called out through the phone that lay abandoned on the ground.

Dust and debris swirled right at me. I was about to be swept away in a gust of moon dirt and particles, but I couldn't move. I cried out, "Olivia! Olivia!"

My vision was gone after that. I couldn't see anything. I was somewhere, but nowhere at the same time. Like a voice on an answering machine. I was in the hospital. I heard monitors beeping, feet rushing up and down the halls.

Someone outside my door spoke about me like I wasn't there. "Blown pupil. The aneurysm explains everything. Doubt we'll be able to save the eye."

"She was repeating a phrase over and over again when they brought her in. 'Olivia Moon'. Does that mean anything?"

"Maybe her emergency contact. I'll check."

The voices outside my room quieted to nothing. Olivia is in the moon. I glimpsed her face just before I stopped seeing. She was soaring toward the cyclone, using her body to block it from dragging me off. I think Olivia is the real protector. The woman on the moon is a worm waiting to gobble everything up. But Olivia lifted off the ground, spread her arms out wide, and smothered the cyclone before it could get to me.

I wish I could see. I would look up at the sky. I wonder whose face I'd see. Mine or the moon's or Olivia's.

# A Rose for Brescia

Snip!

Brescia sat up in bed and listened.

Snip!

She closed her eyes and trained her ear. Maybe the south side, she couldn't tell for sure. But someone was outside on her property. They were stealing from her garden. Again.

Snip!

Brescia flung the covers off, sprung from bed and straightened her nightgown in one smooth motion. She ran from her bedroom to the staircase and jumped over the banister, landing quietly on the balls of her feet. She crouched, waiting for another sound, another clue to guide her.

*I know you're here.*

Brescia waited another beat, letting her pulse and breath quiet almost to nothing.

Snip! Snip!

Brescia spun herself around. The hardwood floor afforded her bare feet no traction. She sprinted down the long hall to the back side door. The perpetrator was in the garden by the fountain. She would catch them this time; she was determined.

She'd lost too much already. She wouldn't let them get away with anymore of her soil, seeds, or stems.

"I got you now!"

Brescia burst through the door leading out to the patio. Right in front of her a dark figure hunched over a bush and dropped flowers onto a white cloth on the ground. Silver blades flashed in the moonlight. *A weapon, shears or a garden knife.*

Brescia didn't hold back. Her first blow landed between the neck and shoulder of the trespasser. "Get out of my garden!" she yelled, rearing back to strike again.

A second blow was lost to the quick movement of the trespasser. Brescia's fist slipped through the stretchy cloak hiding their identity. Her fist fell straight into the stiff, sticky grass.

She pushed off the ground, growling , determined to fight. Then her eyes fell to the cut flowers on the ground waiting to be retrieved. The cloaked one followed Brescia's eyes. They both lunged for the roses.

"Oh, no you don't!"

They both scrambled toward the scrap of cloth, each trying to reach it before the other one. Brescia was almost impressed with the thief. Their movement was fluid, quick, steady. But Brescia was just as fast, just as smooth. She avoided an open palm blow by darting under her rival's arm and returned a swift chop to her opponent's side. She didn't see the blade of the shears coming down into her shoulder.

The shock of being stabbed dazed her just long enough for the thief to snatch up the roses and leave the garden running, albeit slowly.

"Dammit!" Brescia sank to one knee, out of breath. For weeks now someone had been sneaking into the garden and taking clumps of soil, rose buds, and stems. Brescia reached for the tool, but couldn't get her fingers on it. Blood trickled down the back of her arm. Numbness tingled all the way down to her fingertips.

"Let me help you."

A soft voice and heavy floral scent filled the night air.

Brescia turned toward the rose bushes. This time a tangled figure of green leaves, stems, and thorns stood an arm's length away. A head of fat fragrant blossoms shook slowly.

"Ebony, I tried to protect you."

"You did, but you've gotten hurt in the process. Here, let me help you." Ebony stepped behind Brescia and placed a leafy hand on her shoulder and one around the entry wound. Her leaves rustled in the slow breeze.

"Mmm." Brescia inhaled the heady scent swirling around. "Ebony?"

"Yes, Bre?"

"I think I'm going to—"

"Pass out. Yes, I know."

Ebony removed the gardening tool from Brescia's shoulder and dropped it on the ground. She crouched down and scooped Brescia up in her arms careful not to aggravate her wound or prick her with any thorns. "Let's get you inside."

Ebony walked across the yard with Brescia nestled close. Vines crept along after them and covered the ground. They climbed across the patio furniture and crawled up the sides of the house after Ebony closed the doors. Darkness deepened as the greenery completely covered every window, door, and vent. They shimmied into every crack and crevice, some even stretched down into the chimney and up through the sinks.

Once the house was ensconced in total darkness, Ebony exchanged her natural look for her previous form. Her human body felt odd after so long.

Brescia's eyes fluttered open. She strained to see in the darkness, but she made out the rough silhouette of Ebony's face and body.

"Shh. Don't try to speak." Ebony pressed Brescia closer and carried her upstairs. She crossed the threshold of Brescia's bedroom and placed her on the bed.

"Don't go," Brescia said, reaching up. "I've not seen you like this for a long time."

"It's dark. You only see what you want to see."

"No. I see you, Ebony."

The roof sighed under the weight of leaves and thorns. The vines outside grew thicker, spreading across the window then on top of each other blotting out any small traces of light. Ebony's doing.

"You can darken the entire house. Blind me with thorns, whatever. I'd still see you."

"Save your energy." Ebony backed away from the bed, but Brescia stopped her with a hand on her wrist. "You need a bandage for that wound."

Brescia slowly let her hand slip from around Ebony's wrist. She watched the shadowy form disappear into the hallway. Behind drowsy eyelids Brescia saw the scene she always held at the back of her mind.

Ebony standing at the edge of the garden under the archway covered in bright purple bougainvillea, her cream lace veil whipping behind her in the breeze, and her smile outshining the sun.

Brescia walked toward her, the butterflies in her stomach offering to fly her down to where she stood. *This, this is it. The perfect moment.*

"Give me your hand."

"Yes, yes." Brescia's lips pushed the words out effortlessly.

"Give me your hand. Brescia, you're dreaming. Give me your hand."

Ebony's voice brought her back to the present. Her eyes, weak and straining still, opened to Ebony taking her pulse.

"Hold this while I clean your wound."

Brescia gripped the bundle of washcloths Ebony handed her and shifted forward.

"You don't call me sweetheart anymore. I miss that." Brescia tucked her head to be level with Ebony. She was desperate for eye contact, but Ebony refused, focusing on her task instead. The sting of antiseptic made Brescia jerk free from Ebony's hand. "Why don't you come to me like this all the time?" It was normally as a wild tangled mass of flowers that Ebony appeared.

"Because... because you shouldn't have done this. You shouldn't still want me like this."

Brescia's entire body stiffened, she pulled away. "How was I to know spreading your ashes would result in this? I just wanted a little piece of you near me. I didn't think—"

"About what I wanted? About my wishes?" Ebony stood quickly moving away from the bed.

"Ebony, please... Don't be upset. We are together now."

"Are we?" Ebony's face contorted. Thorns undulated

beneath the surface of her skin, leaves sprouted along the right side of her neck, then shriveled away. "You are obsessed. I'm a ghost. A plant based ghost living in the garden. Someone stabbed you tonight with gardening shears."

"I know. I know." Brescia rose from the bed and stepped directly in front of Ebony. "I am obsessed. I couldn't keep you safe before. So I have to do it now. Keeping you safe and near is all I want to do." Brescia nuzzled her face in the space between Ebony's neck and shoulder. She inhaled the floral perfume and kissed her chin. "We are together now."

\* \* \*

Ebony eased out of bed, careful to not wake Brescia. A few drops of rose oil dabbed behind Brescia's ears deepened her sleep and would keep her from following. The vines covering the house remained in place shielding her movements. Her abilities to manipulate the natural world grew stronger every day. Ebony was conflicted though. Being with Brescia again complicated her plan, but she hadn't been able to resist her kisses and gentle, coaxing touch.

The breeze on the patio was much cooler than before. Ebony braced against the wind. Her darkening petals dropped off as she paced back and forth thinking about what needed to be done.

"Psst. Over here." The cloaked figure moved swiftly toward Ebony.

Moving as quickly and quietly as she could with the wind rustling her leaves, Ebony grabbed the figure by the arm and dragged her to a dark corner of the patio. "Give me one reason not to strangle you right here."

"What? What did I do?"

"Are you kidding me, Bianca? Earlier. I told you to come for the roses and dirt, not stab my wife." Ebony yanked the hood down from around Bianca's head. "You could have killed her."

"It was a flesh wound. She'll be all right." The shorter woman jerked free of Ebony's grasp and stepped back. "What do you care anyway? She's been holding you hostage here in this garden ever since the funeral. If I didn't know any better, I'd think you didn't want to leave her after all."

"Patience! Rushing is the reason we're in this situation in the first place."

Bianca hung her head. "I know. It's my fault. You were rushing to meet me. It's my fault you died."

Ebony's memories were mingled with that of the garden, but she remembered leaving the house in a hurry, trying to get out before Brescia got home. She'd tossed her bags in the back seat of the car. "I'm on the way," she said into the phone. "Be ready. We have to leave tonight."

The delivery truck struck the driver's side door the moment Ebony backed into the street.

"If Brescia had just spread your ashes across Lake Eller, none of this would have happened."

"Don't blame her. How could she have known? How could any of us have known?"

Bianca slipped the hood back over her head. "What's done is done. You have a choice to make. I've stolen enough soil and roses over the past three months for this to work. You said you're getting stronger. You can leave her and come be with me."

"She's still mourning. I don't know if I should leave now."

"Are you serious!" Bianca's pointed finger didn't have the effect it should have had. Ebony's thorns formed a tight circle all around her face like a mouth jutting out ready to fend off Bianca's threat.

"Lower your voice, she'll hear you. And put your little finger down." Ebony paced back and forth at the edge of the garden. Blades of grass orbited around her ankles. "Just give me another night to think about this."

Bianca folder her arms over her chest. "Another night. Just one more?"

"Yes, just one more."

"No. No more nights. No." Bianca left the garden without another word.

Thorns pushed up all over Ebony's body. She plucked her rose petals off by the handful and threw them to the ground. Her leaves shed in clumps and blew across the yard. Now what was she to do?

Ebony turned toward the house then stopped herself. She couldn't go back inside and pretend nothing had happened. Her guilt wouldn't let her. The vines formed an elevated bed against the patio's south wall and pulled Ebony into it. She stared up at Brescia's bedroom window all night considering what to do.

\* \* \*

Morning came with bright sunshine. The vines covering the house had retreated sometime in the middle of the night. Brescia hadn't stayed in bed long nor had she questioned

Ebony's not being there. The floor was a mess with rose petals and browning leaves. She'd have to sweep them up later.

After her morning workout, Brescia called her sister and asked her to come over. It had been a while since they'd seen each other.

"We can have iced tea out in the garden. Wait 'til you see what I've done out here."

Before her sister arrived Brescia put out a cheese tray with fruits and nuts and fluffy croissants. She placed a single red rose in the center of the table. Two tall glasses filled with ice and lemon and peaches for tea. The umbrella over the table would shield them from the sun as they talked.

Finally her sister made her way out to the garden. She walked slowly across the grass to where Brescia waited.

"Bre, what's going on? Everything is on fire. I could feel the heat from the front porch."

Brescia looked around slowly. The fire had engulfed the rose bushes on the outer and inner edges of the garden. The grass was scorched. Even the patio furniture was starting to melt. Brescia picked the single rose up off the table and touched it to her face. The delicate outer petals absorbed the tear coasting down her cheek.

"Sometimes you just have to burn everything down to the ground and start over, sis. I'm letting go. "She smiled and stood. "Have a seat, Bianca. Let's catch up." Brescia pulled out the chair across from her and poured her sister a glass of tea. "That's a nasty bruise on your neck. What happened?" The ruffles of Bianca's white dress fluttered like leaves in the wind.

# All the Light There Was

*I want to go back to light.*

*There has got to be a way to get back there,* she thought. Across the sunroom, light poured in obliterating everything directly to the left of the windows. Soma stared, letting her eyes water from the intensity of the light. She could see little bits of past days, months, years collecting in that whiteout space of pure sunshine. There had to be a way to go back, to get back to the time when she felt most herself. Back to the beginning.

When was that? What did that feel like? Had she been there all alone? She'd have to figure those things out first. Or maybe there was some formula, some mathematical equation to get back what she sensed she'd lost. It felt heavy, monumental and yet she'd gone on living. Not one hundred percent this or that, but an amalgamation of who she was, who she could be.

All the promises to never lose herself gathered in her belly like too much water. Over and over again she'd lost out to desires she didn't understand, crippling needs that thrust her into the arms of men and women who had their own agendas. There was always an overly jubilant thought that everything would work out in the end.

The chuckle in her throat came on so strong it surprised her with real tears. *Everything would work out in the end,* she thought again and another short laugh lifted her.

"Yes. In the end."

Soma unwrapped herself from the fraying throw she'd snatched from the couch when she moved to the sunroom for a few moments of quiet. It was the black and gray striped number with the eagles soaring over a calm landscape of mountains. She looked at it now convinced it held answers she should use to get back there, wherever there was.

"Hey, Ma, can I go to the… You been crying?"

Reagan bent down to look at her. He'd grown so tall in the last six months. He towered over almost everyone at his school, students and teachers. He made himself shorter, slouched to ease the awkwardness, to make people around him comfortable.

"Stand up straight. No, I wasn't crying. The sun is extremely bright in there. My eyes were watering. Where is it you're wanting to go?"

"Oh, there's a party on the beach. Down by Surfside Cafe. Some friends from school."

"Which friends?"

Soma smoothed her hands over Reagan's shirt collar. He'd grown muscles too. He was more of a man these days than a boy. He cut the grass and took out the trash without being reminded.

"Shoshanna and her sister and Edwina from band."

"Mmhm." Soma hummed and grinned.

"What's that look? Can I go?"

"You're just so handsome." Soma grabbed her son's face and looked into his eyes, two wide, open pools of brown light. "Yes, you can go. Take Ruddi if he feels up to it."

"He's upstairs studying, I think."

"Ask him if he wants to go. And take your phone with you. Answer if I call, please."

"Thanks, Ma."

Soma accepted the quick one arm hug Reagan offered then listened to his heavy footsteps on the stairs. They stopped in front of Ruddi's bedroom. She strained to hear their voices. Soma imagined Ruddi smiling, jumping up from his desk, and grabbing his jacket. *Go have a fun night out,* she willed her younger son, but the quick beat of footsteps down the stairs told her he had declined.

"Ruddi didn't want to go, Ma. I'll be back before midnight." Reagan rattled off his goodbye as he descended the stairs and his weight carried him right out the door.

Soma walked through the living room folding the blanket back over the couch as she moved past it. She would dart upstairs, poke her head into Ruddi's room, ask him if he wanted anything special for dinner since it would be just the two of them tonight, then make some tea. But the sunroom called her back.

*You know how to go back.*

Particles of light floated all around in that one corner by the windows. Soma stood completely still. The sunlight was hypnotizing and strong. She remembered being awed by the light streaming in through the skylight at her granddad's house. She'd lie on the floor directly underneath the opening in the ceiling and watch the particles of dust dance in the tracks of light, the warmth on her face holding her in an uncomplicated embrace. Time stopped.

"The light held me so close."

Soma put her hand out and closed her eyes, pressing against the air until she felt resistance. Behind her lids flashed colors like the panels of a stained glass window, no particular images, just saturated pigments, red, blue, and yellow with the veins in her eyelids outlining small shapes. In her chest a weightlessness so powerful it almost took her breath.

*Yes. Yes. This is it. Let go.*

She wanted so desperately to name the feeling rising in her, but she only slightly remembered it. She stood there with her eyes shut tight, on the cusp of an outburst. She didn't hear Ruddi calling her from the stairs.

"Ma? Maaa? Ma, what's for dinner?"

Soma opened her eyes. She was disappointed she hadn't gone anywhere. Soma whipped around finally acknowledging her younger son who stood leaning over the rail of the staircase.

"Huh?"

"Dinner? What are we having?"

"Oh, uhm. Pork chops?"

"Ooh, yeah. Okay. You need any help?"

That was Ruddi. Helpful and considerate. Unafraid to offer his time and energy. He was smart and quiet too, and a host of other good qualities. He'd recently won first place in the science fair for creating a new type of small-cell solar panel out of recycled materials he and his brother found around the neighborhood. He was her soft one, her sensitive one. Where Reagan liked to be out exploring and making friends, Ruddi liked being close to home, close to Soma. Soma loved both her boys. Ruddi was just more like her; they had more in common.

"I'll get things started. You can come make the salad in a bit, okay?"

"Okay."

Ruddi started back up the stairs when Soma stopped him. "Hey, Ruddi?"

"Yeah, Ma?"

"I love you."

"I love you too, Ma." Ruddi blushed and grinned before running back up to his room.

Soma turned her back to the sunroom and crossed over to the kitchen to start dinner. The sunlight followed her there and perched on the ledge of the window touching the window-box garden Ruddi had helped her build. Basil, mint, and cilantro were just starting to sprout. The plants' tender necks stretched toward the sun so naturally. They knew how to get at the thing they needed most. Soma wanted it to be that easy for her too.

Soma moved around the kitchen not really thinking about what she was doing. She pulled pans from drawers, set out spices on the counter, and turned the oven on to preheat, but then she just stood in front of the window staring out, not focused on anything in particular and gripping the edge of the sink like she'd fall over if she didn't have something to hold on to.

"I'm slipping," she murmured softly. "Slipping away. Slowly. Slowly slipping away."

A blue and black butterfly danced across the deck in the warm sun. From the window its movements looked like a choreographed battle. Wings flap forward, wings push back, rise higher, higher. *Take me with you.*

The pork chops on the counter needed her attention. Soma turned away from the dance and busied herself with rinsing the meat, then with sprinkling just the right amount of tenderizer on each thick cut.

"No time for a marinade really." Soma forced herself to focus. "I'll bake them, nothing fancy. I might be able to make a chutney with this stuff." Soma had pulled out two apples, raisins, almonds, honey, salt and pepper.

Soma sliced the apples into manageable pieces for their old food processor. "Ow! Dammit!" The knife slipped, cutting her fingers. So much for focus. The warm sensation of blood pulsing to the surface stilled her movement. Soma watched the blood darken as the air hit it.

The small bathroom off the living room had a first aid kit. Soma would clean her cuts and dab on some antiseptic and continue cooking. *Continue. You must go on. But in what way? How?*

There was little light in the bathroom, but the small space held her like light. Soma closed her eyes. She saw light inside of her, pushing against her cells and borders, wanting to get out. *Focus on that. You are the light. You are the light.*

First one foot, then the other was off the floor. Soma floated effortlessly. She drifted a centimeter or two to the right and back to the left until she was steady, her body a particle of dust moving with the room's current.

*What do I call this,* she wondered, trying to balance her here and now with the there and then feeling. *What do I call this? How can I keep this?*

"Shh," she hushed her thoughts. She could figure out when, what, and why this moment was later. The actual floating didn't compare to the internal sensation swelling and contracting all throughout her body. It was like being filled with warm fizzy water and having it travel in and out of each vessel and capillary leaving behind a tingling clean feeling.

*Yes!* She floated in place. This was the beginning. She could feel there was more. More light, energy for her to see and feel and live in. She wanted it all. In her mind she could see the orb, a tiny glow growing toward her. She was passing through it. Then it was passing through her.

Quick footsteps on the stairs interrupted her. Her feet touched the ground and she opened her eyes. She cleaned and bandaged her fingers and went back to the kitchen.

Ruddi rinsed a head of lettuce at the sink. Soma watched his movements. Flicking off the water, shaking the lettuce, drying his hands. He was efficient, unconcerned with anything else at the moment.

She needed to be more like that. Focused, dedicated to one thing at a time. *The light. Guide the light through me.*

After dinner she focused inward despite her drowsiness. The chops and the spicy chutney sat heavy in her gut. *You are the light. You are the beginning.* Her mind opened up again, made a connection to the orb that moved in and around her. She watched with unblinking eyes as she traveled back, deep within herself to the warmth, the security of light all around. She felt fat and heavy with it.

"Mom, you're glowing."

Soma looked over at Ruddi. He'd turned off the TV and

crawled up on the couch beside her. She was reminded of how strangers would tell her that very thing when she was pregnant with him. "You're glowing." How they would even reach out to pat her stomach.

"Thank you, sweetie."

Soma ruffled Ruddi's thick braids with her hand and patted his cheek.

"No, I mean you're *glowing*. Look." Ruddi poked her arm with his index finger. The glow, the size of a small oval at first, spread down to Soma's wrist and fingers. "Does it hurt?"

Soma shook her head. She raised her arm and waved out in front of her. The glow moved back and forth with her.

"What is it, Mom? What's happening to you?"

Soma stood without answering her son. The glow, the light, followed her everywhere she moved. It grew brighter with each step she took until she wasn't stepping at all. She was floating again. She closed her eyes. *You are the light.* She focused with all of her strength, all of her power.

*We are the light.*

Soma turned around, her floating body moving like prethought, fluid, languid. Ruddi hadn't moved from his place on the couch. Though an indention of a smile shifted his features. Had he spoken? Soma stared and blinked.

Ruddi stretched out his palm to show the pulsing glow at his fingertips.

Soma felt all the air leave the room. The glow disappeared. The light left just as it had come. All the lights in the house flickered. Soma crashed down to the floor. She cracked her elbow on the end table, shattering it in two places.

"Mom!"

Ruddi rushed over and crouched down beside her.

"It's all right," Soma sputtered in between sobs. She tried getting to her feet, but couldn't. Bright blobs of light collided behind her eyes.

"Don't move, Mom. I'll call an ambulance."

Soma sobbed harder.

Ruddi stayed by her side. He teared up when she looked up at him. He stroked her hair. "It's okay. It'll be okay."

The paramedics loaded Soma into the ambulance and checked her vitals.

"Are you experiencing any dizziness? Nausea?" The female paramedic's voice seemed far away.

Soma's reaction time was slow. She focused on Ruddi's face as he hovered near the paramedic's shoulder.

"Ms. Nellis, did you experience any head trauma?" The paramedic held a penlight in front of Soma's face, moving it from eye to eye, side to side. "Just follow the light, okay?"

Soma did as the paramedic asked. She looked into the light, but kept Ruddi in her peripheral.

*We are the light. We are the light.*

# Feeling Blue

Claire stepped off the bus at Third and Walsh. She was one block away from her apartment and beyond ready to be home.

"Almost home. Almost home."

Her discounted Cole Haan flats clacked across the pavement, but they also pinched at her toes, scraped at her heels, and suffocated the side of her foot where an arch should have been. She couldn't tell whether or not she was flexing her feet anymore because they were numb in places. Her entire day had been a conscious effort to not think about how badly her feet hurt, but she'd failed miserably. Half a size too small hadn't made a difference to her when she saw the shiny brown and gold leopard print gems at Carolina Thrift, but now she desperately wished she had a smidgen of wiggle room.

Claire thought about slipping the flats off and walking the short distance barefoot, but the scattered bits of trash that included glass, nails, needles, a Whopper wrapper about to take flight, and what looked like runny dog poop on the sidewalk kept her too tight shoes firmly on her feet.

"You gotta make better decisions, Claire."

"I know. They were just such a good deal I couldn't resi—" Claire stopped at the corner just before crossing the street and looked around. There was no one nearby. She looked back behind her. No one.

"Girl, your feet are killin' you. Got you talking to yourself."

"Huh?" Claire whipped her head around again searching for the voice talking to her.

"Up here, ma! Ha-ha! Look at you! Those shoes do look good, girl."

Claire stepped back from the corner and looked up at the building. A giant mural of a woman painted in bright colors looked down at her. Unruly blue locs danced across the dingy brick. An opaque crystal jewel jutted out from her forehead like a unicorn's magical horn giving off energizing beams of light. The blue-haired woman was stunning—a honey rich mahogany diva with oversized heart shaped bamboo earrings and fuchsia lipstick. Even with eyes hidden behind rainbow lens sunglasses, Claire could tell this woman did exactly as she pleased against her red, orange, green, and ivy print backdrop. Claire instantly felt intimidated.

"Did you just talk?"

"Claire, don't act like you're surprised! Everyday for the last six months you've gotten off that bus and you've seen me and we, you know, do the lil' head nod, acknowledge each other and go on 'bout our business."

Claire thought about that for a second. Yes, she'd seen the mural before, but had never really thought about it beyond how colorful it was. She never thought about *it* noticing her.

"I see you walking around deep in thought, looking like you don't have a friend in the world. Well, you got me. I'm here to lift you up. How come you never stand around to chat?"

"I don't know. I didn't think about it." She shrugged, feeling silly for not having considered talking to the beautiful image. "So, how are things?" Claire stepped closer to the building.

"Yeah, girl, come a little closer. I know how you run. Come on. Bring it in. You need a hug."

Claire looked around to see if anyone was watching. Still, no one was on the street, at least not nearby. A few people strolled behind her on Tanner Street toward the bodega. She took a few steps closer, tentatively raising her arms out to the side.

"Been awhile since you had a nice, good, long hug, huh? Yeah, me too. Feels good, don't it?"

Claire nodded. She mashed her face and body up against the building and sighed. Emotions she didn't know had been hiding bubbled up in her chest. Fear and sadness and loneliness. She was drained. It had been forever since she'd had a hug, since she'd even thought about wanting or needing one. She was skin and body contact deprived. The body pillow in the middle of her bed just wasn't cutting it. She couldn't even remember who her last hug was. Her ex, maybe? Six months ago?

Claire didn't want to think about Laney, but just like she was suddenly embracing the side of a dusty building, she was suddenly recalling the last time she talked to her girlfriend. She had gone over to Laney's to reclaim forgotten items she had stashed in a drawer. It was over between them. Laney needed space, freedom, all the things people who stopped loving you said they needed when they couldn't bother with you anymore. But after Claire gathered her things and turned to leave, Laney had wrapped her arms around her, pulled her close and took a deep breath almost as if she didn't want it to be over, like she didn't want Claire to go but couldn't change the outcome.

Claire felt warmth radiating from the building where her body touched it. The blue-haired woman was actually hugging her. And it did feel good despite the strangeness of being outside hugging the wall of a building for the entire world to see.

"Wow, yeah, it does feel nice. Human to, err, wall contact." Claire stepped back and looked at the woman. "How'd you know I needed a hug?"

"Claire, I know tons of things. I know that you hate your job and you're dilly-dallying with your art. What's that about, yo? You're stubborn as hell, girl, and you haven't been giving yourself enough credit for half the things you do. Why you haven't been asking people for help? Girl! Oh! And I know that your feet are killing you 'cos you make bad purchases in the name of fashion and looking good for other people."

Claire sighed. Her cheeks were burning from the awkward, scrunched way she was holding her mouth. The mural was right. She didn't even know what a Cole Haan was until a girl at work was carrying on about how amazing they were.

"Yeah, I know. It's just that—"

"What?" Miss Blue Hair's tone changed and she shifted her shoulders, closing herself off to any excuses Claire tossed her way.

"Well, you know, things get in the way. I gotta make a living, pay the bills. Art doesn't speak to people the way it used to…" Claire thought about what she was saying. An art piece three stories high was literally talking to her on the street making her point moot. She folded her arms over her chest. "I'm busy, I get busy with things. And—"

"And bullshit!" Miss Blue Hair leaned forward and sneezed out the word twice. "Ooh! Excuse me. Goodness. I'm allergic to bullshit excuses from talented and fully capable people who aren't living up to their own standards, living for everyone but themselves." She dabbed at her nose with a handkerchief she pulled from the backdrop then let it fall to the ground by Claire's aching feet.

"Easy for you to say, Miss Unicorn Blue Hair Art! Look at you! You're gorgeous, larger than life. Someone's dream come to life on the side of a building. How do I compete with that?"

"Oh, honey, you can't compete with all of this. Not in a million." Blue gave herself an approving once over. "You have to make time to do the things you love! Speaking of love, what happened with you and Laney? She was crazy good for you."

Claire swished her lips from side to side thinking. "I… I don't know actually. Laney, she was like a dream, you know. And dreams, they go flat sometimes."

"Are you calling me flat? Oh, no she did not!" Miss Blue Hair pursed her lips and started unclipping her earrings. "Now you listen to me, Claire. Maybe you feel like now isn't the right time to be kicking through walls and taking risks, but that doesn't mean you get to quit. What happened to the girl who used to write and paint and draw and sing and dance all over the place? Where's the woman that wanted to fall in love and create things? The one who'd rather run barefoot than wear some too tight name brand shoes, which, you know is a metaphor, right?

"What do you mean?"

Claire looked down at her feet. The pain was both searing and numbing at the same time. If there had been any room in the shoes at all, her pinky toes would have fallen off and rolled around inside by now.

"Claire, Claire, Claire. You're wearing shoes you don't particularly like and are enduring physical pain simply because you are too afraid to do your own thing. You think the people you work with care that you wore some shiny shoes with someone else's name on them? Shooot!"

"Um, so, that's not a metaphor—"

"Hey! You know what I'm saying. Ain't no sense in it, sis. Why you holding everything in?"

Claire backed toward a fire hydrant and leaned against it. She lifted her left leg over her right knee and slipped off the circulation-stopping shoe. She rubbed her foot.

"Ooh," she crooned. It felt good to wiggle her toes and actually feel them for the first time since that morning. But the contentment was short lived. Claire put her shoe back on and prepared to continue her walk home.

"Hey, where do you think you're going?"

"I gotta get home. I—"

"Well, wait a sec. I wanted to give you something."

"What is it?"

"Hold your horses, hang on. Let me fish it out of my pocket." Blue reached down into her pockets pulling out almost every kind of kitchen utensil, two headbands, a handful of yellow golf pencils, some Jolly Rancher candies, and a long strand of confetti colored beads. She let everything fall to the ground making it rain around Claire as she kept looking.

"Ah-ha! Here we go." Miss Blue Hair pulled out a small black notebook and a fat potpourri sachet.

"What's this?" Claire took the notebook and sachet, looking at both.

"That notebook belongs to Laney. She dropped it last week and has been going crazy looking for it."

"And the sachet?"

"Reflection dust."

Claire looked from the sachet to Miss Blue Hair then shifted her neck. "Is this glitter?"

"Ha-ha!" Miss Blue Hair tossed her head back as she laughed hard. Her locks swung around stirring up a swift breeze. "Can't get nothing by you, can I? You used to love glitter, remember? It's magic! Go on."

"Thanks." Claire put the sachet in her pocket and looked down at the notebook. "How do I—"

"If you don't take your behind home and change out of those shoes… You probably got hammer toe by now."

The walk home wasn't as painful as it could have been. Claire's feet hurt, but she had a lift to her step now. She wanted to get home, change out of the Cole Haan shoes she'd probably never ever wear again, and figure out her life.

Claire kicked off her shoes as soon as she had the front door open and stepped inside. She went straight to her closet and pulled out the art supplies she'd shoved to the back. She grabbed a sketchpad and her favorite pencils and tossed them on the bed. After staring at them for a few minutes Claire went to stand in the shower. She needed to think. Questions swirled in her head, all in the blue-haired woman's voice. 'Why and why not' echoed the loudest. Why had she let Laney go without at least asking her why? Why hadn't they communicated better? When did she decide to give up on art, on everything? And why did it take a piece of art on a building to push her to want answers to these questions?

Beneath the hammering water of the showerhead Claire couldn't hear the questions anymore. The only sounds were the water running down over her body and her whimpering. She didn't know why she was crying. Those same emotions she felt when she hugged the building came up again, but stronger this time. She missed Laney; she missed the parts of herself that she had been ignoring. She pounded her fist against the wall and yelled into the showerhead. The muffled watery sound of her voice made her want to cry more.

Claire stepped out of the shower and wrapped herself in a towel. She wiped the fog from the mirror and stared at her reflection. Reflection dust. Hmm. The glitter was on the dresser in her room. She tucked the ends of her towel in tight and went into the bedroom where she plucked Miss Blue Hair's gift up and held it in her hands. Why had she been walking around in shoes that hurt her feet all day? Why was she walking around hurting, not asking for help?

Claire tugged the end of the string holding the pouch closed and opened the top. Flakes of yellow and orange glitter shimmered back up at her. She shook some out into her palm. It was cold like it had been in a dark place for some time. Claire took a deep breath in and brought her hand up near her lips.

"Make a wish."

\* \* \*

Claire almost hoped Laney wouldn't be home, that her car was in the parking lot of her apartment complex only because she'd gone somewhere with a friend. Claire knocked lightly. What if this blew up in her face? What if Laney opened the door only to slam it shut? Or if someone else answered the door? A new lover, her replacement.

Claire heard footsteps approach the door. Her fingers started to tingle and for a second she considered running back down the stairs to hide in the bushes so Laney wouldn't see her running to her car.

"Hey, Laney. How are you?"

Laney smiled wide. "I'm okay. I'm good."

Claire and Laney took in the sight of each other without saying anything else.

"I know you weren't expecting me, but I found your notebook."

"Oh, wow! I've been looking everywhere for this. I can't believe you found it. Thank you!" Laney reached out pulling Claire into a firm hug. "Thank you for bringing it over."

"Of course."

Claire stood in the hug trying to absorb as much contact as possible without being the weird ex-girlfriend. It just felt so good to hug a real person, this person. She didn't want to let go. Laney's skin was warm cinnamon and acrylic paint fumes wafted around her.

"This is going to sound so strange, but I was thinking about you today." Laney pulled back, but just an inch so she could meet Claire's eyes.

"You were?"

"Yeah. I mean… I often do."

"Really?"

Laney nodded. "How are you? You look good. Wanna come in?" Laney stepped aside to make room for Claire to come through the doorway. "Don't mind the mess. I was working on some drawings."

"I see. Looks like you've been keeping busy." Claire scanned a few half drawn images on the coffee table as she made her way to the couch. "These look promising."

Laney sat down next to Claire. "I've missed you. What's going on in your world?"

*Oh, not much. Talking to images on buildings, punishing myself for all sorts of things.* "Oh, you know, same ol', same ol.'"

"No, I don't buy it. How are you, really?"

"Um, well… uh," Claire sighed deep, unable to speak actual words. The flutter in her chest calmed a little when Laney touched her arm. "Not that great. I've lost something."

"Do you know what it is you've lost?" Laney looked straight into Claire's eyes, holding her gaze and peeling back her layers.

*Myself, you, time, energy.* Claire swallowed and cleared her throat. "I… Can I use your bathroom?"

"It's in the same place as before. Go right ahead."

Nothing had changed in Laney's apartment. The small dining table they'd painted green was still covered in posters, mail, and fast-food napkins. The Bob Marley tapestry hung from a hook in the hall above the end table with incense and a black candle.

Claire shut the bathroom door behind her quickly and let her head fall against it. She wanted to leave, sprint out the apartment. She didn't know why she thought she could come here and take six months worth of emotional baggage off like a pair of shoes. If she left now, she could save what little bit of dignity she had left.

But what would the blue-haired woman say if she saw her cowering in the bathroom?

*Tsk, Tsk, Tsk.* Claire channeled what she thought Miss Blue Hair would say. *Get back out there. Tell Laney how you feel.*

"But I don't know how I feel. I'm so confused. About every single thing."

Two soft knocks on the door brought Claire out of her panic.

"I'll be right out."

Claire stood in front of the mirror willing her image to change. She trembled knowing she needed to be someone else, someone stronger, bolder for a change. Unsure of how she'd accomplish the transition, she wet her hands with cold water and patted her face.

Laney was sitting on the couch. She'd cleared a space on the table for two cups. "I made tea. You still like peppermint?"

Claire nodded and sat down next to Laney. Her breathing drowned out the words she wanted to say. She stopped and started several times, then finally forced the words out. "Do you think we could start over? Us? Paint over the parts we didn't quite get right the first time? Even if just as friends."

Claire reached out and grabbed Laney's hand with both of hers. Until she touched Laney, Claire didn't realize she was shaking. "I feel so foolish. I'm so bad at this."

"I think you're doing just fine." Laney squeezed Claire's hands then gathered her in a loose side hug. They sat together quietly soothing each other. After a while they eased into conversation, gently probing each other for the latest news from their lives.

"Looks like you're getting ready for a show or something. I see you've been busy creating new stuff." Claire picked up a few sketches from the table when Laney took their cups to add more hot water.

"Yeah. I've had a handful of commissions. Just some small stuff."

"That's exciting." Claire picked up one last sketch from the table. It had been buried at the bottom of a pile of half drawn faces and shapes and experimental lines. This sketch had been filled in with color so vibrant it felt alive in Claire's hands. She stared at it, easily recognizing the blue-haired woman from earlier. A huge open smile stretched across Claire's face as the image in her hand winked and nodded. Claire couldn't wait for Laney to come back from the kitchen. Whatever had made her doubt herself was lifting away. She turned her head toward the kitchen and projected her voice for Laney to hear.

"I'm happy for you."

# Cosmic

Esme sipped her coffee while scanning her assigned area, sector B475. She could see the incoming storm from Mars a few thousand miles away pushing particles in her direction. By the time they got closer she'd be handing her shift over to Sunny Jr. for the morning rounds. If it hadn't been for Sunny, Esme might have failed her galaxy exam a fourth time which would have put her back to a lower class of star and she wouldn't have the job as a Sky Patrol officer. With both her mom and dad being board members of the Council of Celestial Entities she would never have heard the end of it.

They weren't pleased with how many times she had to take the exam in the first place. They thought it made them look bad. Ernestine couldn't stand the idea that others were talking negatively about her Esme, calling her a fumehead and a druggie.

'What are you doing with your life, Esme? When are you going to make us proud, Esme? Patrons of the galaxy look to us, Esme. We are an esteemed family. These types of things follow you.'

Where exactly her mother didn't say. Esme was tired of hearing about the almost shame she'd brought to the family. Thank the heavens for Luna. Her positive outlook always seemed to bring Esme out of her funk and her recommendation helped get Esme this first assignment. Plus, Luna marrying the earth girl and stretching the very fabric of outer space made for much more salacious talk than her own inability to calculate the rate of star creation.

Esme took another sip of coffee as she jotted down coordinates in the logbook and listened to calls coming in over the radio. There was a bulletin out for a star gone missing a day ago. But Esme hadn't seen or heard anything. Most everything was off in distant sectors.

"Nothing doing," she said mimicking the way Sunny Jr. called out a slow shift. Patrol went so much faster when Sunny worked nights with her. He was so funny with his impressions of the planets and galaxy gases. His impression of Saturn always made her laugh until she couldn't breathe. "Guess who put a ring on it?" he'd say in his deep voice while bouncing his shoulders up and down. He made Beyonce's choreography look easy. He was back on days now, which was a bummer for Esme, but Sunny was on the fast track being related to the sun and all.

Something caught Esme's eye in area 22. Clusters of rhythmic cloudburst floating up into the sky. It wasn't smoke signals. It looked more like wishes and they were climbing fast. She toggled her radio frequency to call base station.

"Patrol 111 to base. This is Esme."

"Go ahead, Esme. What you got?"

"Not sure, Jamie. Can you zoom in on sector B475

subsection 22? I think I got a coupla' Wish-I-Mays, getting a little rowdy."

"Roger that. Zooming B475 sub 22."

Esme watched the clouds dissipate as Jamie scanned the area. Her mouth fell open in awe. She'd never be one of those celestials who didn't feel the wind knocked out of her when she viewed the majestic beauty of her world. There were so many layers and colors and precise degrees of differentiation that it would take several lifetimes to enjoy them all. A moment of spiraling could take you to the height of out of this world wonder. Now that she wasn't fuming all the time she saw so much more. Whoo! Black holes were a helluva drug in themselves.

"Oh, yeah, Es, you called it. These kids are making wishes like it's last call at the Little Star."

"What do you know about the Little Star?" Esme smacked her lips. She hadn't been there since her last failed exam. That's where she went to drown her sorrows and fume out without judgment and get her groove on when she was feeling lonely. A grungy, hole in the wall type bar where all the misfit and uninitiated celestials clung to life. But she'd kicked the fuming habit cold when she thought she was going back to being a ball of low-grade particles. She'd cured herself of everything save the occasional bout of loneliness. For a second she wondered if that cute bartender with the green swoopy bangs and the waxing moon tat next to her mouth still worked there. Before she could get too lost thinking about how close Esperanza's little moon had been to her mouth Jamie chimed back in.

"Ha ha! I'll never tell," Jamie replied with a high-pitched

giggle. "So, what do you want to do about the wishers, Es? These kids are in your jurisdiction."

"Uh, well, let's…" This was only the third time Esme had had any kind of trouble on her nights doing patrol. The only citations she'd given so far were for small infractions, attempting to gift a star, donating constellations in memory of, nothing major. She had a few scientists scared for talking smack about Pluto. She couldn't officially give them a ticket, but she made it seem like she would if they kept it up. Pluto was a close friend and she couldn't just let that kind of bad mouthing slide. Not a planet? Like hell. Luna was always bringing up the need for punishment for the little sickos that thought mooning her was hilarious, but there was nothing Esme could do about that. It wasn't even an infraction. Wishing on stars though. That was a big no-no.

Bright stars were known to be totally into themselves all the time. Like Sirius the king of 'look at me, look at me,' and Rigil who for some reason now wanted to be called Cyril because it sounded like the kind of name a rock star would have. When they sparkled and caught every sad lonely human's eye those helium heads didn't know how to act. Once they heard all that star light, star bright business there was no reining them in. It's as if they got completely hypnotized by their own image until they collapsed in on themselves in an ugly dramatic drawn out death. Reviving a star was nearly impossible to do, though it had been done before, once or twice in an attempt to keep the constellations from having to go through auditions for replacements.

But the worse part, the reason for the infraction on wishing, was that these stars have the power to grant wishes.

Not all wishes. Nothing like 'I wish I could fly' or 'I wish I was a billionaire.' Those types of wishes went straight to the Fates and Supernatural Committee— they had an office in Sector J660 that they rented for cheap from Sunny Jr.'s uncle. But the more basic wishes, things like 'I wish I could lose weight' or 'I wish Shania would notice me' they could do and with very little planning. A twinkle here and a twinkle there and it was done. Wish granted. It usually didn't last long, a few months max, but the stars granting those wishes usually mucked up a lot of plans and got folks in a lot of trouble (especially if, say, Shania was already married or in a committed relationship— sheesh). Next thing you know folks were cursing at the stars, shaking fists at the heavens and what not and that's just not the kind of publicity the friendly skies needed... ever. So Sky Patrol was to stay on top of the Wish-I-Mays and keep the self absorbed celestial beings from tossing too many wishes around.

Esme knew Jamie was waiting for an answer, but she was having a hard time coming up with one. She thought back to her training, but her mind was swirly. What would Sunny Jr. do?

"Let's, uh, let's hit them with 60,000 lumens direct from center."

"Heck, yeah! Blind the little snots." Jamie's key panel beeped in a high tone as she punched in the order. "Alright, here goes."

Subsection 22 lit up like a baseball stadium. Pulsing light radiated down covering everything in shocking white light. Jamie flashed the kids three times in rapid succession.

"Whoa! Do you think that was too much? I didn't want

to literally blind them, just take away the desire to look up here." Esme had to adjust her night vision; she could only imagine what the fanfare looked like from below.

"Nah, I think they got the hint," Jamie chuckled and ran a full sector scan, sharpening any audio feeds she could pull up.

"So, you liking dispatch?" Esme tried a bit of small talk while the scan processed. She didn't know Jamie all that well, they'd only been on call together a handful of times, but she seemed great, always willing to help.

"Oh, yeah dispatch is where it's at. I like the challenge. Keeps me alert."

Esme hoped the scan would finish soon so she could go on with her patrol. If all was quiet for the rest of the night, she was going to stream the latest season of Atlanta Housewives off a nearby satellite while she kept an eye out on things.

"Oh, no!"

Jamie's tone didn't give Esme confidence for the rest of her night. "What is it?"

"The scan picked up major heat signals, rising fast."

"What does that mean?"

"Hang on. The scan isn't quite finished yet. But I've seen this before."

"Come on, Jamie, what is it?"

"Shit! Those kids. They got fireworks."

Esme groaned internally. An unscheduled firework going off could bust the night wide open and cause major problems. There were protocols for this kind of thing. Starting with three month's advance written notice to set off fireworks.

"How did this go from a Wish-I-May situation to a Fire-in-the-Sky?" Esme babbled while she cracked herself open and pulled out her fire retardant star shell. "I'll check for any nebulas in the area." Esme locked onto the emergency zip line system at her docking station and began moving down the quadrant corridor.

"Alerting satellites and clusters."

Before any preventative actions could fully be put in place the first firework screamed its way into the atmosphere. A blue sizzler kissed the sky spreading out like haphazardly thrown streamers ripping into the skyscape.

"No, no, no," chanted Esme as she maneuvered in and out of quadrants pulling up safety gates and locking down safety glass to protect the homes of her friends, family, and community.

"Damn, Es, you're fast when shit hits the fan."

"Thanks, but tonight was supposed to be low key," she retorted back, zipping to the next section as more fireworks made their way up. The night sky filled with bright magenta shimmers, green towers that turned gold, and red starburst clusters. "Hey, can you put up a halo until I get all these safety gates up? Starting to feel the heat up here."

"Ooh, no can do. Halos got recalled last week. Faulty bindings."

Esme shook her head in frustration. Did she miss that in the patrol bulletin? It didn't matter. She hustled to get the protective gear up and around all constellations in her area. She might have been a fumehead in the past, but there was no way there would be massive damage on her watch.

"Hi, Esme. Looking good."

Esme snapped around to see Spica strolling by in a leather mini skirt and black glitter top. She nodded in the femme's direction but kept locking gates into place. She didn't have time to chitchat, though she wasn't exactly mad at the way Spica looked in that skirt. Her legs were incredible, all shiny and toned. There was a rumor going around that she and Spica had hooked up the last time she'd been at the Little Star. Esme hardly remembered. She didn't know if she felt embarrassed or proud of that. She decided she didn't have time to think about it right now.

"Hey, Spica. You should probably get inside. We got fireworks."

"Oh, all right." With a smile and a twinkle the leggy star moved along toward the Virgo constellation, but not without adding a little something extra to her walk.

"You like easy girls, huh?" Jamie chuckled into her mic.

"No... I... Spica isn't easy... I mean... Now's not the time." Esme didn't like being laughed at. She felt embarrassed. Focus on the job, she told herself turning her attention back to her task.

"Incoming," Jamie yelled.

Fireworks flared all around popping and cracking open. Damage had already started to accumulate. A nexus of gas crystals floating en route to Scorpio caught fire. Esme rushed over to aid them. As she squelched them with cold cloud particle blankets, Esme felt the urge to fume out long and hard on purple gas until all the tension eased from her body and nothing mattered. It was so much easier to float through space without any specific worries, twinkling and burning oxygen but she knew that would only upset her parents again.

The fireworks didn't seem to stop. One after the other they kept coming. If she wasn't smothering an innocent bystander with a cloud blanket, Esme was dodging stray firework ash.

"It's like they have an arsenal down there. It's been forty-five minutes and they haven't let up yet." Jamie sounded worried. "I'm running out of atmospheric layers to push."

"That's it! Jamie, call Sector B478 for back up. I'm going down there."

"Esme that's a bad idea."

"Bad ideas are my specialty."

Nothing Jamie said persuaded Esme from diving toward Earth. In her mind she knew Jamie was right. She should have continued to her patrol area and put out fires, but she was pissed. She wanted to go to the source and give what for to those responsible for the mayhem going on in her sector. There were rules and now that she wasn't ignoring them, Esme was responsible for making sure that others followed them. With a ticket book firmly tucked under her helmet, Esme set course for a direct approach to ground sector L77, directly below her patrol area. Esme felt wild and out of control flying through the atmosphere so fast. The air on her skin felt hard and electric as it pressed firmly against her star shell. Her night vision picked up other stars and particles whizzing by as she descended. Esme got distracted by the shades of black as she passed through each sky layer.

Gorgeous, she thought, wishing she had a moment to float from layer to layer testing its density and opaqueness. Maybe when she was off this weekend she'd cruise around.

The closer she got to the ground the more nervous she felt. Gas bubbled in her stomach and her coffee threatened to come back up, but this had to be done. Plus she had something to prove. Once she saved her community from these firework misfits she'd show everyone that she wasn't just a screw-up fumehead. She'd be a hero. Other stars would look up to her. She would be the guest of honor at the Starlight Parade and get to ride in the center of the Calabash Nebula float and wave to everyone. The thought of her mother saying, 'I'm proud of you, Esme,' after all this time would close the gap in their relationship. Mouthing the words to herself while picturing her mother's face made Esme vibrate. She closed her eyes for a moment to hold on to the sensation. Her mother. Proud of her again. It would be epic.

Esme opened her eyes still smiling, but the smile didn't last long. An irregular chunk of black atmospheric ore tumbled into her path and crashed right into her star shell. Before she could adjust to the hit Esme was falling, fall-ing, falling.

"Jamie! Jamie, I need help," she cried trying to push herself back into the flight path and out of the way of other falling rock. There was too much debris and the hit she'd taken felt like it had done serious damage to the protective star shell that also served as her cruiser. Metallic liquid streamed out of one side of the small vessel and smoke plumed out the back.

*Braap!* Another huge piece of ore cut into the nose of the star shell. Air poured in through the gaping hole in the cruiser whipping the vessel all around and threatening to suck Esme out.

She was no longer on course. Her speed increased out of her control and there was nothing she could do to pull up. They didn't prepare her for this in patrol training. Probably because she wasn't supposed to go AWOL and fly to Earth in the first place.

Patches of light flashed all around. She couldn't make out what part of the sky she was in anymore. Somewhere near the outer layer, she guessed.

Just before she hit the ground she knew for certain that Jamie was right. It was a bad idea for her to go down to Earth to stop the fireworks.

"Jamie, can you hear me? I'm in trouble. Last known coordinates somewhere north of Nebula CC1201. Jamie, I'm hit! I'm hit!" Esme didn't know if her message went through. She wasn't sure about much of anything as her lungs tightened from lack of air and she became dizzy. The star shell was severely damaged and quickly deteriorating around her.

"C'mon, c'mon." Esme looked for something to grab onto. If she could attach to some particle or beam of energy, she could bind into it and become collision ready.

The cold ground crashed into her before she could transform into an appropriate mass for the atmosphere. A fine mist of dirt and dust rose up in a pale puff around her.

Her radio fell off and bounced a few feet out of reach. Static crackled in and out along with what sounded like Jamie's voice.

"Es… Ca… yo… hear me? Es… ?

Esme shook her head trying to gain her sense of balance.

She couldn't tell if she was up or down, standing or sitting. A jagged scrap of star shell cut deep into her thigh. A high-pitched screech from her earpiece pierced through her head and disrupted all of her thoughts. "I've been hit," Esme whispered, then blacked out.

✳ ✳ ✳

"Hello? Anyone in there? Hello?"

Esme's eyes fluttered open. How long had she been out? It was still dark out and quiet. The cool air brushed over her skin making her fingers tingle. When her eyes focused on the face hovering above her she was confused and startled.

"Jamie?"

"Sorry. No Jamie here. I'm Kurtisha, you can call me Kurti."

Kurti's voice sounded like a soft vibrating bell. Her face looked like too much matter stuffed into its human package. The deep black emptiness of her eyes made Esme question if she was awake. Esme tried to nod, but the left side of her face stiffened. It hurt to move her neck too. She looked around. There were plump round bushes and sturdy trees, patches of green all around. A sweet smell hung in the air. Esme recalled from her exam that Earth air had a sugary scent. She was on Earth. She remembered her trip through the sky, falling, falling, falling until, *thunk*, she'd hit the ground. She looked up at the sky. The soothing dark and intermittent twinkle of lights was familiar and calming. An urgency to get back where she belonged struck her right in the stomach.

Esme pushed herself up on her elbows. Gravity introduced itself quickly. No longer light and compact Esme realized every movement would take effort. Wet thin lines ran down her right arm and the sharp pain in her thigh registered.

"Don't move. You're injured."

"No, I'm all right." Esme tried to get to her feet. She sucked in her breath as she realized standing wouldn't be so easy.

"No, you're not," Kurti said. "Please, just sit for a moment. Gain your composure. It looked like a rough landing."

"You saw me fall?" Esme settled on her left side to take pressure off her thigh. Her mind was still racing. She needed to get in contact with Sky Patrol and Jamie.

"Oh, yeah. I thought you were an airplane at first, then a shooting star, now I don't really know what to think." Kurti was kneeling down beside Esme assessing her injury. Her orange hair stood out straight from her head as she reached toward Esme with her hands. Waves of wrinkles rippled across Kurti's skin. "Um, what's happening?"

"Sorry about that. I'm highly charged. It's perfectly safe."

"Are you sure?" Kurti looked down at her hands. Her veins pulsed up to the surface of her tightening brown skin.

"Positive," Esme said lightheartedly. A beat passed with Kurti still eyeing her changing skin, then she laughed.

"Oh, I get it! Positive. Highly charged."

"Kurti, listen, I'm Sky Patrol. Here's my badge." Esme slipped her triangular identification out of her pocket and showed it to Kurti. The shine on it made Kurti pull away and shield her eyes. "I was on a mission to stop some kids shooting off fireworks when my cruiser was damaged. I need to contact base. But I've lost my radio and my cruiser disintegrated."

"Sky Patrol? Fireworks? You're not making sense. You must have a concussion." Kurti's face twisted up with concern. Her black eyes shimmered.

"No, please listen. About an hour or more ago some kids were sending up wishes, and then they started shooting off fireworks. I have to stop them so they don't destroy the sky community."

"So, you really are a star or something. Whoa!" Kurti froze for a moment and gave Esme a more thorough looking over. "Do something celestial."

"Huh? I showed you my badge. You can feel the electromagnetic pulse. What other proof do you need?"

"I want to see something out-of-this-world. Something celestial."

"Please, Kurti, I obviously need your help."

Kurti stood up and folded her arms. "I need proof."

"Forget it!" Esme found this needing proof beyond the badge insulting. She didn't need any human to help her. She was Sky Patrol. She was a high level star. She personally knew the Sun's nephew. "You humans are all alike. No wonder this place is going to pot." With newfound vigor Esme got up on both feet. The pain in her leg only throbbed now and she was determined to complete her mission. A nearby stick looked like a good implement to help her walk.

"Wait! I'll help you."

"It's too late." Esme hobbled toward the few buzzing streetlights in front of her.

"You don't know where you're going."

Esme stopped and turned back to look at Kurti. "I'm a damn star. I think I can manage."

Kurti laughed then jogged a few paces to catch up. "There's a diner a few blocks that way," Kurti pointed. "I bet you can stop in there to *phone home,*" she said shrinking her voice and waggling her fingers in the air.

Esme didn't say anything. She just marched on in the direction Kurti had pointed out. It was the same general direction her gut was urging her toward.

"An honest to goodness star. Wow. I can't believe it. Actually, I don't believe it. So, what's it like living among the clouds?"

Esme adjusted her grip on the stick and moved as quickly as her injury would allow. She had her ears tuned for any frequency that would allow her to make contact with Jamie or Sky Patrol Headquarters.

"I studied astronomy in school," Kurti kept right on talking. "Fascinating stuff. But I know there has to be more to it than constellations and darkness, right? Isn't there a gateway to heaven? Or is it a stairway?"

A wave of uneasiness swept over Esme. Kurti's tone was starting to sound strange. She was babbling, but with a curious urgency. It was odd she asked about a gateway to heaven. There was a rule at Sky Patrol.

*Rule 36: Do not engage in discussions of heaven, superpowers, or aliens with non-celestial beings.*

Looking over her shoulder Esme noticed Kurti's shadow moving differently from her form.

"You can tell me. I can keep a secret." Kurti let out a note of nervous laughter.

As Kurti was laughing Esme received a shrill pitch in her ear that almost crippled her further. She stopped in her tracks, holding tight to her makeshift cane.

*Esme? Esme, are you there? It's Jamie. I'm in stealth mode. Plink twice if you can hear me.*

As subtly as she could, Esme tilted her head up toward the sky and opened her eyes as wide as possible. Two pulses of high voltage light shot out. *Plink, plink.*

*Esme! Thank the heavens. Okay, listen carefully. I see you. And who you're with is bad news. Kurtisha M. Rove is a wolf in sheep's clothing. She's literally a star hunter. She was responsible for the wish storm and the fireworks. It was a ploy to get one of us down there. She's done it before. We think she's got Martine.*

*The star that went missing? Jamie, I'm injured.*

*I know. I've got help on the way. Both Sunny and Luna are coming for you. There's a satellite station a few clicks north of where you are. It looks like an old 50s diner. Get there. Get inside. You'll be safe.*

*I'm headed there now, but Kurti is not backing off. She started acting strange a few miles back. She's asking questions, trying to get info. I should have known something was off.*

*Esme, be careful. She can't get inside the station, it's protected. But she might try to use you to get inside or to get to someone else. Some of our people are in there. You're not the first to go hurdling through the atmosphere to stop her damage. We were able to lock onto your signal when you sent your maide. I tracked similar instances of unapproved fireworks in combination with other infractions. She's tried everything in the book.*

*But I got taken out by crumbling ore. What does that have to do with Kurti? What does Kurti Rove want?*

*What doesn't she want? To eat the universe one star at a time. To get by the gatekeepers and attack heaven maybe. She's been at this for eons.*

*Jamie, I'm scared.*

*Don't be. I got your back, kid. Do what you have to do. Just get to the diner.*

"You're awfully quiet. Galaxy got your tongue?" Kurti laced her fingers together and let her large arms bounce in front of her. "Obviously you're mad I wouldn't help you back there. I thought you were being weird, okay, trying to play me for a fool. Let's start over, huh?" Kurti skipped in front of Esme so they'd be face to face. She extended her hand. She had such large hands all of a sudden. "Here on Earth we shake on things."

Esme didn't like the way Kurti's thick eyebrows twitched or the way only one side of her mouth formed a smile.

"How 'bout I buy you a cosmic coffee once we get to the diner."

"What makes it cosmic?"

"Wait and find out."

Esme saw in Kurti's eyes she was walking straight into a trap. Kurti had another thing coming if she thought Esme would just roll over and let her take whatever she was after. She reached out her hand to accept Kurti's offer. "Sure, you can buy me a coffee." When their palms touched Esme sent as much electricity as she could through Kurti's palm.

"Yow!" Kurti stumbled back flapping her hand in the air.

Narrow eyes honed in on Esme.

"Sorry. This injury has me surging. I can't seem to control it."

The stench of burned hair filled both their nostrils.

"Right. It's fine. It didn't hurt that bad." Kurti waved her hand down by her side to hide the impact. "C'mon, let's get to the diner."

"Hey, you never mentioned why you were out tonight." Esme leaned heavily on her walking stick. She was getting tired. The jolt of energy she summoned to shock Kurti took from her own supply. Gravity wasn't helping much either. Her body weighed her down. Fat drops of sweat gathered at the back of Esme's neck and rolled down her back.

"Would you believe me if I said stargazing?" She let out a deep chuckle that sent chills across Esme's back and down her legs.

"Stargazing, huh?" Esme saw the 24-Hour Diner sign a few yards ahead. If she harnessed all of her energy, she might be able to run and throw herself at the door. If any of her people were inside like Jamie said there were, they would see her and let her in. She'd need a diversion to get far enough away from Kurti to keep her from getting in right behind her. The diner looked out of place; it was alone at the corner of a two-way street. This could be a trap in itself. But both her gut and Jamie had guided her there. She had to trust, if not herself, Jamie.

"I'm feeling… woozy. I need to rest."

"What? The diner is right there. You can see it, can't you?"

Esme moaned and made a wheezing sound through her nostrils. "Oh, man. Everything's going dark. I'm gonna pass out."

"Oh, no you don't. I got you." Kurti wrapped her arm around Esme's waist to help hold her up.

Esme swung her elbow into Kurti's side as hard as she could. When she staggered back Esme landed another blow with the walking stick. The hand-to-hand physical training Sky Patrol had put her through had seemed ridiculous at the time, but Esme was thankful for it now. Esme raked the end of the stick across Kurti's jaw. Kurti fell to the ground completely off balance. Esme's use of the walking stick opened a window for her to limp the distance to the diner.

*Jamie, I'm almost to the diner. But I don't have much time. Kurti won't stay down for long. I'm running out of energy.*

*Esme, get inside! Hurry! We're almost to you.*

Esme saw the lights on inside the diner. She could also hear Kurti catching up to her. Heavy footsteps pounded the ground sending tremors out beneath her feet. She knew if she looked back she'd be lost forever. She didn't want to be lost.

"Let me in! Let me in!" Esme banged her fists on the glass door of the diner. She stopped when she realized the lights were on but there was no one inside. None of her cosmic predecessors had lasted long enough to be rescued. Peering into the diner Esme saw only heaps of sparkly ash. On top of a bright saffron pile of ash lay a half burned trainee nametag. The remaining letters spelled out MART. Esme let her forehead clank against the glass. "I'm so sorry." She needed Jamie, Luna, and Sunny more than ever.

"From stargazing to star grazing now," Kurti stood right behind her, huge and hulking. Her human figure was transformed. Tufts of wiry orange hair sprouted over her entire body. Her belly glowed blue like she'd swallowed a thousand galaxies for lunch. Only the narrow eyes made her recognizable. "I'm going to eat you!"

"Wait!" Esme pressed herself against the glass door trying to will it open still. She was thinking of a way out, but hadn't come up with it yet. Where were Luna and Sunny and Jamie? "Can I ask you a question?"

"So, now you want to talk? No. I can smell the fear in you and it's making my mouth water."

"What happened to those guys in the diner? I thought we were safe in there?"

"They were safe. But being trapped inside a small space can make a celestial go crazy. They made their decision."

"Still you have to admire that even in death stars are beautiful. Look at how they shimmer still."

"Do you know how hungry I am?" Kurti stalked closer.

"Why didn't you just take me back in the field? You had me right where you wanted me."

"I trapped another star yesterday. I wanted to have you both. Dinner and dessert. I needed you to open the door, but I guess he fizzled out like the others."

Esme tucked her chin onto her chest. "I finally got my life on track and I screwed it up again."

"What are you mumbling about?"

"Nothing. I — I thought I was going to be someone important. I thought I could make my parents proud for once."

"I'll tell them how delicious you were." Kurti licked her lips.

"Would you mind if I fumed a little? I really don't want to feel what's about to happen."

"There's no escaping this. I won't be fooled."

Esme ignored Kurti's dripping lips and closed her eyes. She didn't have any readymade gas on her but she knew how to produce it. With clenched fists she squeezed her core until her internal spark ignited. The cool purple gas started to flow and wash over her. The combination of gas and tears stung her eyes but she didn't stop fuming.

"Hey, what are you doing? Stop that!"

The gas formed a voluminous cloud and began to seep under the diner door. It slowly started to fill the space near the front of the building. Kurti snatched Esme up in her big hands and shook her. "Stop it!"

It was too late. Even if Esme passed out completely she'd continue to fume. She was counting on that and the right amount of gas slipping under the door to cover the space between the door of the diner and the first lump of star ash on the floor. A chain reaction could bring at least one of the other stars back to life depending on when they had fizzled out.

Esme saw bright yellow lights just beyond Kurti's monstrous head. She was fading out. If there was only some way to let her parents know she'd tried, this wouldn't all be for nothing. "I'm not a fumehead, mom." The words fell out of Esme's mouth just as Kurti opened her jaws and took a bite.

"Put down the star and put your hands up!" A booming voice echoed through a megaphone. "You're surrounded!"

Sunny Jr. and a small patrol unit turned a 100,000 watt spotlight on Kurti. Luna and Jamie rushed to Esme's side. She lay limp and crumpled on the ground.

"Esme, please, please don't go. Please." Jamie fit an oxygen mask over Esme's mouth and checked her vitals. The wound from Kurti's bite was crystallized, purple and shiny. But her electromagnetic pulse was weak, almost non-existent. "Luna, do something!"

"Not much I can do, Jamie. She held on as long as she could. We didn't get here in time." Luna turned away toward the diner. She didn't want Jamie to see her tears fall.

After securing Kurti in sunstrobe handcuffs and loading her onto the celestial prison van, Sunny Jr. joined Jamie and Luna. "How's our girl?" Sunny looked from Jamie to Luna. "She's gonna be okay, right?"

Jamie stared at the ground.

"No. No. We can bring her back. Right, Luna? Luna?"

Luna's voice failed her. She shook her head and leaned against the diner window.

*Thwack! Thwack! Thwack!*

Luna jumped away from the building. There banging against the window were two reconstituted stars. Martine and Lil' Libby. Martine waded through the remaining purple gas and unlocked the door.

"Am I glad to see you guys!" Martine gulped in air before speaking again. "Where's the girl who fumed us back to life? That was quick thinking using the gas reconstitute method. I'd forgotten that from the galaxy exam."

"Esme reinstated you guys?"

"Yeah! It was pretty amazing." Lil' Libby stretched her neck looking for Esme to thank her.

Sunny Jr. smiled half-heartedly. "She always got that equation wrong on the exam. But she got it right this time."

"Yeah." Luna nodded. "She did good. Her folks will be so proud."

# Demetria's Nature

"Aunt Sarah, are you sure? I don't want to have a chest full of hair grow back if I pluck this thing."

"Yes, I promise. Now get on with it."

Demetria stood in front of the bathroom mirror naked from the neck down to her waist. Telling Aunt Sarah about the tiny, pale, thin hairs that occasionally grew in between her breasts and how they'd gotten darker and thicker seemed like a good idea at the time. The two of them were close. They talked about everything. Demetria didn't think too much of telling Aunt Sarah about the one freakish hair that had sprouted out of a deep pore and stood straight up like a spider leg caught in a window. Growing hair in new places was all a part of this stage in her life.

But Aunt Sarah sprang up off the couch and looked at Demetria like she was the answer to life's greatest question. She started saying crazy things. "Oh my goddess. My niece is the one. I knew our family was special. I knew it."

Now Demetria was in the bathroom about to yank the hair out of her chest because Aunt Sarah said this was a defining moment, not just for Demetria, but for their family, the world.

There was a bit of a snicker from the other side of the bathroom door. Aunt Sarah might have been pulling her leg. But what did she have to lose? She was going through the change whether she liked it or not.

"It's just one hair. Nothing is going to grow back all weird," she said, encouraging herself. She was nodding in the mirror. The motion made a bit of skin beneath her chin wiggle and she stopped nodding. She stretched out her arm and a sagging length of skin waved gently back and forth then finally stopped after a short time. Demetria placed both hands on her belly, gave it a playful nudge, and watched it ripple like a disturbed mud puddle. She looked back at her reflection again. "It ain't so bad." A crooked hook of a smile slipped onto her face. After all she still felt like herself and for the most part she still looked like herself. Her reflection winked.

Demetria rummaged through her makeup bag for tweezers. She meant to pluck that irritating hair right out of her chest fast, without much ado.

"Here goes."

At first attempt, the hair just dodged her every move. She'd come at it straight on and the little thing would duck right under the sharp ends of the tweezers. Then Demetria angled the tweezers to come in from underneath, but the hair coiled like an unruly nose hair on an eighty year old man, once again avoiding being plucked.

"What the cuss?" Demetria tried to snatch at the hair, sneak up on it, grab it with her pointer finger and thumb, but it just wouldn't stand still. "For the love of mother nature," she hissed, growing more and more frustrated. That was the moment the thick, black hair spoke to her... sort of. It coiled and straightened three times in rapid succession making a *boing, boing, boing* sound, like something you heard in a cartoon.

"What?" Demetria leaned down toward her chest and the hair did it again. Coiled and straightened and sang out, *boing, boing, boing.* This time Demetria could have sworn she understood what the hair was telling her to do.

She eyed herself in the mirror for a long time then cupped her breasts and slowly pulled them to either side. Her chest lifted, and right down the middle her dark brown skin begin to perforate. Her chest slowly opened up as if someone had designed her left side to easily come away from the right. As the split grew wider Demetria tried to peer inside. At first she saw nothing but lightness. No blood, no tissue, no bones. Only lightness. Warm, yellow-orange lightness that spiraled deep into another dimension. Then a bit of cool fog slowly drifted out and clung to the air.

"How's it going in there?" Aunt Sarah sounded like she was right outside the door.

Demetria's mouth hung open, but in the mirror her reflection grinned. She jumped back. The fog continued to flow out of her chest and started to sink to the floor. It was fragrant, filling the bathroom with a heavy rain aroma and she was reminded of her visits to the mountains.

After the fog, a robust wind spilled out of her chest. It whipped and whirled about the small bathroom taking her shower curtain for a ride along the metal curtain rod. The wind cozied up next to Demetria's ear and whispered, "Damn, girl, where you been keeping your fine self?" That sent a chill of excitement down her back and smacked her right on the behind.

A yellow-green leaf floated out on the last windy whisper. Then another and another after that tumbled down and fell at her feet until there was a pile. Demetria listened to their bright young voices as they played chase around her ankles. "Auntie, play with us! Play with us!" Demetria scooped them up in her arms and tossed them up into the air. They giggled and fluttered through the air enjoying the attention and showing off.

A silky vine covered in soft white hair slithered out of her chest and writhed against her belly, wrapping itself around her heavy thighs then up her back. "Baby, you still got it. It never left and it never will. Meet me after dark for some sensual healing tonight." The vine kissed up the back of her neck, around to the side of her face, then planted a tender kiss on her lips. "Mmmhmm."

"Oooh!" Demetria shrieked when a small, colorful bird flew out of her and flapped around the bathroom before landing in her hair. "Oh, little birdy, what are you doing? No, no, no. Get out of my hair." Demetria looked like a bird flapping and shooing, but the bird wriggled down deep and made itself comfortable as Demetria squirmed. She looked at herself and now the bird in the mirror. Normally, she didn't like birds because their beady eyes made them look calculating and mischievous. They always looked ready to peck your eyes out. This bird, though its eyes were small, looked calm and kinda punk-rock with all its blue, red, green, yellow, and pink feathers on its head and wings. The jet-black line above its eye was the kind of smooth look Demetria had never been able to capture with eyeliner. Maybe she could learn a few tips and tricks from this multicolored little creature. "You can stay… for now."

The skin immediately on either side of the opening began to glow like sunlight originated right there deep within her. The warmth felt good at first, like taking a stroll on a beach at the perfect time. Then the heat became overwhelming. She was like a human oven. Flower blossoms sprouted on her shoulders, the backs of her legs, and down the front of her body. Bright orange, white, and red blossoms dripped nectar down her front and back. It all pooled in the roll above her hips and in her bellybutton. Sweat mingled in with the nectar making her sticky and uncomfortable.

As if on a timer, a refreshing waterfall gushed out of her chest and created a whirlpool around her, rinsing her of all the blossoms' thick juices. She was left refreshed and smelling deliciously fragrant.

"Demetria? Everything okay in there?" Aunt Sarah knocked on the bathroom door.

"Uh-huh. Everything's fine."

Demetria's teeth chattered. The cooling waterfall had left her chilled. When she sneezed snowflakes fluttered down all around her. "Burr." She slid out of the jumper completely and grabbed her robe off the back of the bathroom door and wrapped it tight around her.

*Boing, boing.* The hair was dancing up and down again.

"What is it? I don't understand."

*Boing, boing, ba-boing.*

"Oh, right!" Demetria cupped her breasts with both hands again, this time pushing them together. Her skin closed with a golden seam.

Aunt Sarah was standing with her head cocked toward the door. Leaves and fog and water rushed out as Demetria opened it. Her aunt's eyes grew wide and she smiled with all of her teeth showing. "I knew it! I knew it! A goddess in our family." She sank down to one knee in worship.